LOVE IN EVERTON

write you a love song

fabiola francisco

books by
fabiola francisco

Dear Reader,

Thank you for picking up Knox and Ainsley's story! Welcome to Everton— a small town hidden in the Wyoming mountains where cowboys rule, gossip runs, and love wins.

I am so excited for you to read the first story in this series and meet the people from Everton.

Knox may be looking to hide out in his hometown, but that's not easy to do when you're the resident celebrity and a country music star hiding from a scandal. When he unexpectedly meets Ainsley, he starts to second-guess everything that he's running from.

I guarantee your trip to Everton will be full of feel-good romance, lots of swoon, and small-town charm. This is just the beginning!

XO,
Fabiola

dedication

For my future husband—
if you don't like Frito pie and snowball fights,
I don't think it will work out.

prologue

Knox

The flashing car lights I'm anxious to leave behind are a blur as I speed down the highway. I can't drive fast enough to escape my past. I scrub a hand down my face, the other tightening around the steering wheel as my knuckles whiten.

The radio is silent. I don't want a reminder of the one thing that stole everything from me. The swooshing of the other cars I race past is enough music for my ears. The pelting rain on my car adds the only drumming I need right now.

An angry breath moves through me, and I blow out air from my lips. All I can think about is her. Her and the pain in her eyes that mirrored the same pain I put there four years ago.

It's done.

It was done a long time ago, and I'm the only one to blame.

I squeeze my eyes shut despite my flying speed. I've lost control of everything in my life. Little by little, I gave a piece of my life to a dream I thought would offer everything I ever needed.

Instead, it destroyed me. It destroyed my passion. And now, the media is having a ball with it all, blowing it all up, making mountains out of invisible grains of sand. Enough to hurt both her and me.

I was naïve, and she was strong.

I flick the turn signal and take the exit, the shrilling sound of an incoming call interrupting my thoughts.

"What?" I bark out.

"Where are you?" My friend and manager, Harris, asks.

"You know where." I go to hang up, but his voice comes through.

"Don't do it," he demands.

"You can't tell me what to do anymore."

"Knox, we'll get through this. We'll get a new label. Hell, you're famous enough you can create your own label and release whatever you want," he tries to convince me. This is about more than my music. This is about something bigger than a label, it's about a culture.

"I'm done, Harris."

"When will you be back?" His voice rings with resignation.

"I don't know." I hang up and pull into the airport.

Grabbing my suitcase, I stalk through the doors, cap low on my face and head bowed. I go through security, never glancing back at the city I'm leaving behind.

chapter 1

Knox

two months later

I stare out the glass doors that lead to my patio and out onto the frozen lake behind it. I've always loved this view. When I bought this house six years ago, I imagined a different use for it. I pictured a family running around and holding the woman I love while we sit by the fireplace, talking about our day.

That image is gone now. In its place is an empty house that I haven't visited in far too long.

The woman I love has moved on. I can't blame her. I didn't expect her to wait for me when there was nothing to wait for. I made choices and the consequences have placed me exactly where I am in this moment.

My career is at a crossroads. I never thought that at the age of thirty-five, I'd be in the middle of a scandalous divorce to a woman I never loved and only married because of my career. A power couple, my ass.

I got tired of acting. I got tired of pretending I was happy when each day I'd lose more of myself and my love for making music. Time here in Everton will do me good. Nothing beats being home.

"Hey, man." I turn around to see my brother, Axel, standing by the stone fireplace in my living room, his cowboy hat casting a shadow over his face. I didn't even hear him come in.

"What's up?" My hands in my pocket, I walk up to meet him, leaving behind the peaceful view that's keeping my sanity in check. I haven't had this much free time in years.

"How are you holding up?" He rubs his hands together in front of the fire.

"I'm okay." Truth is that for the first time since I've been a kid, I feel lost. I've been in the public eye for years, a country music superstar. People have followed my career since the beginning, and that included my marriage to Amelia. What no one ever knew was that my heart belonged to another woman whose heart I broke the day I chose music over her. Every promise I made her was swept away with the string of a guitar, and now I have to lie in the bed I made.

"You look like shit. Let's go grab a beer." Axel walks toward the door, leaving no room for discussion. While I left to chase my dreams in Nashville, he stayed here with my parents. Small-town living with a huge ranch and enough land for a community to live on.

I grab my hat by the front door and hop into his truck, my focus on the crunching sound of the tires on the snow as he pulls away from my driveway and down the road.

"Have you heard from Amelia?" Axel interrupts the silence.

"She's giving me a hard time with the divorce. She thinks I should pay her more. Something about breaking her heart and being caught by surprise. She's making shit up. She knows we were never happy, it was a marriage of convenience for her as well." I stare out the window.

"What about Reese?" he asks with hesitation.

"What about her?" My jaw ticks as I bark out my question.

"What's going on with her?" he speaks with more confidence, no longer afraid to hurt my feelings.

"Nothing. She's moved on. Couldn't really expect her to wait a lifetime for me when I was off married to someone else, could I?" Doesn't matter that I held on to my feelings for her. She had every right to make a life for herself after I left her. No, I didn't leave her, I asked her to be the other woman in my life. All I wanted was a life with her.

I shake my head and run my hand through my hair, combing back the long, wavy strands.

"I can't blame her." He gives me an apologetic shrug, his eyes focused on the road.

"Me neither. It just sucks. You know what she told me? She tried so hard not to fall for someone like me, but she did just that. She has a man that's starting off his career in Nashville. The only difference is he won't be a pussy like me and let her go. She'll be able to live every experience by his side, not behind closed doors like I asked her."

"You gotta let that go. It happened, and it sucks, but that's life. We make choices and have consequences. At the time, you thought it was the right thing to do," Axel tries to talk me off the ledge.

"Yeah." I drop the subject. I've been back in Everton for a couple of months, and I've stayed mostly to myself. The rumors are flying, and I don't want people asking me if it's true that I cheated on my wife or that the label cut ties because I abandoned my wife. The rumors are already swirling, and they'd never believe me even if I told them it's not as complicated as the media makes it seem.

In reality, I've been losing my passion for music for a year now. The resentment I felt for being manipulated into something I didn't want has simmered for years until one day I exploded. I no longer had control of my life, and that took away my joy. Even the music I loved writing was replaced by songs other songwriters created for me to sing. Their words and emotions were coming out of my mouth all for the sake of a trend.

I run a hand down my face and sigh. Thankfully, we arrive at Clarke's Bar, a town staple. I could use something stronger than beer.

I keep my head down as I walk through the door and take a seat at the bar. Axel is right behind me, letting me take the lead.

"What can I get ya?" the bartender asks.

"I'll have a Sam Adams," Axel responds.

When the bartender looks my way, I say, "Macallan, neat."

"We don't carry that," the bartender says with annoyance.

"What do you have?" I look behind his head at the bottles displayed on the bar wall.

"Johnny Walker." He scowls.

"Fine. Thanks."

"You ain't in the glitzy cities anymore," Axel laughs, clapping my shoulder.

"How can I forget?" I sigh and look out the window at the falling snow. I love my town but being back hasn't been easy.

The bartender is quick in serving our drinks. I thank him and move the glass to my lips.

"Cheers?" Axel raises his eyebrows.

"Yeah, sorry." I tap my glass with his. It's something we've always done since we were kids at home. My parents always made sure to toast before we drank, and that's carried over into our adult lives.

"Okay. I've let you sulk for a few weeks. Now, what's the plan? You're gonna stay here, but don't you have contracts and commitments you're breaking by leaving it all behind?"

"Fortunately, I wasn't working on a record. The label wants to sue me for abandoning my contract, but my lawyer is working on it. I'm sure there's a loophole somewhere. As for my fans, we had a New Year's Eve concert planned, and I'll do that for them."

"So, you're done, done? No more music?" Axel's eyebrows pop up behind the brim of his hat.

I take a long drink of whiskey and turn to look at him. "I used to live for writing songs and performing them. It was a dream I busted my ass to reach. The grass ain't always greener on the other side." I scrub my face.

"Sometimes I wonder what my life would've been like if I stayed here and worked the ranch with you and Dad. If I had married my first high school girlfriend."

"Nah, that life was never for you," Axel interrupts with the shake of his head.

I shrug. "I thought a life in Nashville was for me, and as soon as a label was interested in me, they changed me. Everything was for a business purpose. It didn't matter if I wanted to write songs about home, they wrote songs about love and made me sing it. My success was always dangled in front of me. Could I even say I was successful when it wasn't the authentic me who was shown to the public?

"For fuck's sake, I married a woman I didn't like and broke the heart of the one I loved to make millions. What kind of person does that make me?" The question is rhetorical, but Axel answers regardless.

"At the time, you thought it was the right choice. You were advised that the industry worked that way."

I shake my head. I'm tired of excuses. "I was a stupid kid." It's been eight years since I met the woman I thought I'd spend the rest of my life with, and six since I left her for someone else.

"If you keep kicking yourself, you'll never overcome this."

I shake my head and order another round for both of us.

"Hey, Adam. Sorry, I'm late. The snow started up as I was driving here." I turn to see a blonde woman move behind the bar.

"It's okay, sweetheart. I'm finishing up here and will leave," the bartender, who I now know is Adam, smiles at her. I guess I need a pair of tits to get him to smile. My attitude probably didn't help with how he served me.

She ties a waist apron around her body and smiles at us. "I'm Ainsley. If you need anything, let me know."

"Hey," Axel smiles at her.

"I know you know my name, but he doesn't so I thought I'd be professional and introduce myself," she continues to talk.

"My brother, Knox," Axel tilts his head toward me.

"Well, I *know* who he is. Everyone does." She looks at my eyes and smirks. "Nice to meet you." She reaches her hand out for me to shake.

I look at it for a beat and grab it. "Likewise." Then, I take a gulp of my scotch, letting it warm me. Snow continues to fall, the weather always unpredictable this time of year. It isn't rare for snow to fall in October, but it's been snowing more than I remember.

"Be nice. She's kinda new to town," Axel warns.

"You got a thing for her?" I raise my eyebrow.

"Nah." He shakes his head. "But she's a friend." He mirrors my lifted eyebrow.

I nod and finish off my drink, ready for round three.

"Neat?" Ainsley asks when I signal to my glass.

"Please," I nod.

I watch as she dances behind the bar, serving drinks and laughing with customers.

"She's something else," Axel says, noticing me watching her.

"How long has she been living here?"

"A few months."

I nod my response and turn when I hear my name being called.

"Hey," Eli, my best friend, pats my back. "Haven't seen you around." He smirks.

"What's up?" I stand and shake his hand.

"Just here to grab a drink. Hey," he turns to Axel.

"Hey," Axel juts his chin in greeting.

"Hey, gorgeous," Eli smiles at Ainsley. I can't keep track of all the *Heys* thrown around in the matter of seconds or the way I feel like an outsider amongst my brother and best friend. "Can I get a beer?" He takes a seat next to me.

I squint my eyes as she smiles and shakes her head at him. "The usual?"

"Yup." Eli turns to me. "You've been hiding at home? You could've called when you got here. Been too long. How are you holding up?"

"Needed some time. I'm okay, happy to be here," I tell him. There's no need to go into details in a public place.

"Well, it's about time you came to visit, even if under shitty circumstances."

"Thanks," I chuckle. "The choice was mine, you know?" I shake my head. Gotta love Eli's transparent honesty.

"Yeah, yeah. You must be insane to leave that hot wife of yours." I know he means well, but I grind my teeth to stop myself from saying something I'll regret.

"Eli…" I warn. "You don't know shit."

"Got it," he raises his hands. "Well, you've been missed around here. Younger Bentley isn't the same as you." He points to Axel.

"I'm more fun than this guy."

I laugh at them. It's just like when we were kids. Eli loves messing with Axel.

"Cheers," Eli holds his glass up to us. We join him. "To old friends and new beginnings."

I nod, able to get on board with that toast.

It's nice to catch up with Eli. The more I drink, the more relaxed I become. I leave my self-pity for a while as I join Axel and Eli in conversation and watch as Ainsley's mood affects everyone who comes into the bar.

Clarke's is full of people coming in for a drink and a bite to eat. She knows almost everyone who sits at her bar, personalizing each conversation according to their life, drink order, and even kids.

When I get back into Axel's truck, he looks at me. "What did you think of Ainsley?"

"What?" I meet his gaze.

"Saw you staring," he states with raised eyebrows.

"It's not what you think," I defend.

"Whatever," he shrugs, not buying my excuse.

"I'm not looking for anything right now. I thought it was cool that she's been here for a short time and knows the town so well. People seemed to love her. That's all," I explain.

"Okay." He drops it and turns the ignition.

When he stops in my driveway, he says, "Come by the ranch tomorrow. Don't stay home hating yourself and your life. It ain't worth it." I nod and step onto the snow.

Walking into the house, I add a log to the fireplace to spark more heat and drop onto the couch. I chance a glance at my phone, lying on the coffee table where I left it this afternoon, and see a message from Harris.

I skim it and throw my phone on the cushions. I'm not going back to Nashville, no matter how many times he begs me to reconsider. Nashville is where Reese is, where the memory of what we had lies. It's why I agreed to live most of the time in Los Angeles with Amelia. I thought if I could get far away from the memories, I could move on.

I've never been more wrong.

chapter 2

Knox

"Hey, Mom." I hug my mom as she greets me on the front porch where she's been standing since I pulled into the driveway. "It's too cold to be out, let's go inside." I wrap an arm around her shoulders and lead her into the house.

"How are you, sweetie?" She holds my free hand with both of hers in comfort.

"I'm good. Thought I'd come by and see how things were going here. Get out of the house, you know?" I smile, trying to reassure her I'm okay when she knows I'm not.

"That's good. Come, I have fresh coffee in the pot."

We walk into the kitchen, and I fix us both a cup of coffee before sitting at the kitchen table with her.

"Axel told me you went to Clarke's with him yesterday. Glad he got you out of the house." I nod. "I know this is a hard time, but we all know you didn't do anything wrong."

"Thanks. At least my family knows I wouldn't cheat. I'm tired of the crap. Sorry," I apologize when I notice her glare. "Not crap, attention," I correct my word choice.

"It's part of the career you chose. You knew all the consequences beforehand." She's right. My parents and I would talk about all the possible situations I'd encounter if I became a famous musician. We never discussed an arranged marriage, and I never told them the truth. For all they know, I met Amelia and fell in love with her. I couldn't stand disappointing them.

"Yeah. I just want the divorce to be finalized, so I can move on from all this."

"It will happen. Be patient." She pats my hand. "I don't know what exactly your connection to that young lady is, but maybe a statement explaining why your relationship with Amelia ended will help clear the air."

I shake my head. "I can't."

"Why not?" Her eyebrows pinch together.

"If I tell the truth, the label will sue me. Back when I met Amelia, I signed an NDA that I would never share the real reason we got married."

My mom tilts her head, curiosity bouncing off of her. "What is the real reason?" Concern deepens the wrinkles around her eyes.

I take a deep breath. "You can't share this with anyone," I clarify. "My publicist set Amelia and me up years ago. It was all a publicity stunt to better both of our careers. Her success had exploded in the music industry, and I was getting noticed by fans. Amelia was Pop Music's Sweetheart, and I was the next big thing to hit country music. An unlikely couple that could merge two industries, especially now that modern country music has a pop influence.

"Basically, I was told by the label if I wanted them to record my music, I had to marry her."

"What?" My mom screeches. Her hand lands over her heart as her eyes pop open.

I push back and frown. "Sorry, Mom. I know that's not what you wanted to hear, but it's the truth. I was told it was the only way my career would take off. I know now that wasn't true. Reese was my girlfriend at the time, but we kept it hidden so she wouldn't be pulled into the spotlight. I thought I was protecting her, but instead, I was destroying what we had. However, I don't think the label would've cared if they knew about Reese. I was... am in love with her, but shit happens." I shake my head and shrug.

"I'm surprised, but it all makes sense now. Why the papers are saying you and Reese aren't strangers." She gives me an apologetic smile. Her eyes are still wide in disbelief. I hated keeping this from her and my dad, but it was the only way.

"It's why I left Nashville. I couldn't do it anymore. I kept going against everything I believed in until I had enough and took a stance. After I told Amelia I wanted a divorce, I went to see Reese. She's already moved on. I deserve all of this for what I did to her, but it doesn't make it hurt less. Not just losing her, but losing the passion I had for music and the control over my life. Everything is backward." My body slumps in the seat, my coffee getting colder with each word I speak.

"What counts is that you *did* take your life back into your own hands. You'll figure out what you want in your life and what your priorities are. You just need time, and you need to stop being so hard on yourself." She lifts her head and looks me in the eye with a firm gaze.

"Yeah. Right now, I want to finalize the divorce. That's my priority. My lawyer is already looking at how we can get out of my contract with the label. It's safe to say they are not happy with me and will do anything in their power to keep me for the sake of their egos."

"Well, that won't happen. What does Harris say?"

"He says we can open our own label, and I can create the music I want. Start fresh," I shake my head. "I'm not feeling it right now. I've lost my respect for music, and it will take some time to get that back, if I ever do. It's done more harm than good."

"We'll figure it out, day by day," she reassures me.

"Yeah." I nod. "Dad and Axel are out back?" I ask.

"Yes, go say hi."

I kiss my mom's cheek and walk out to the barn, my breath smoking as I exhale.

I look out at the snow-covered mountains behind the barn, clearing my mind after helping my dad and brother with the cattle. As much as I love this life, I'm no rancher. I can roundup cattle like the best of them, but it's not my passion. I shake my head and grip the back of my neck, massaging a knot that's formed there.

I have enough money that I can take time off and figure out what I want to do next, I'm just not used to having all this free time. I'm used to being out on the road, spending long hours recording, press releases, and appearances with Amelia. I blow out a gust of air, releasing the memories.

"Hey! Lunch is ready," Axel calls out from the back porch. I nod and head over. As I enter the house, the aroma of cornbread and chili wafts around the house. There's nothing like Momma's home-cooked meals.

My dad and Axel talk about work while we eat, my mom smiling between them as she watches their passion. I eat in silence, observing it all and wondering how I can fit back in this town.

"Son, you adjusting to being back here?" My dad looks at me.

"Yeah, I needed this. There's nowhere better than home to reflect and regroup. I was tired of living in LA, and Nashville started to suffocate me with all the media going after me."

"Coming back to your roots always puts things into perspective," my dad smiles and squeezes my shoulder. "Now, what you missed most was your Momma's cookin', wasn't it?" he winks.

I chuckle and nod. "Of course. You don't get this kinda meal anywhere but here."

"Suck ups," my mom states with a roll of her eyes but smiles.

I may be going through a tough time, but I know I can always count on my family to have my back. No better people I want in my corner than them.

♪

Axel: we're going out tonight
Knox: not up for it

**Axel: too bad omw to pick u up so get dressed.
it's the weekend**

I sigh and climb the stairs up to my room. He won't
give up, and I know going out for a drink will do me
good. This town is small enough that we won't get too
wild, but I have to be careful, knowing someone will take
advantage of my being here and sell a story to the
tabloids. The last thing I need is more cheating
accusations, or worse, that I'm an alcoholic. People are
dying to add more drama to my reputation than the
simple truth that I live a quiet life. I've never been one to
live a life of debauchery.

My phone pings with another message, and I'm
about to walk out thinking it's Axel when I see the name
on the screen.

**Harris: Amelia is losing her shit. She went from
crying cheating victim to saying you mistreated
her**
Knox: the fuck?
**Harris: my theory is she feels like without you
she'll lose the spotlight so she's saying
anything to keep her front and center**
**Knox: that's bullshit. i'd never do smoethign
like that.**

My hands shake with anger as I type out the last
message, not bothering to correct my typo. This is
getting out of control and I need to call my lawyer
tomorrow. I want him to find a loophole in the NDA I
signed, because the only solution to this mess is to
publicly share that our marriage was a publicity stunt.

Thankfully, we got that in writing. I don't care if I get the biggest lawsuit handed to me, but I'm tired of this bullshit.

Knox: do you have copies of all my contracts?
Harris: yes
Knox: keep the copies and send me the originals overnight.

I have my own copies, but I want the originals in my possession. I wouldn't be surprised if Amelia's publicist is telling her what to say and how to act. She always loved drama. I warned Amelia once about her, but she wouldn't have it, stating her publicist was the best in the business.

I turn toward the door when I hear Axels' truck and its loud ass engine running outside in my driveway. I grab my coat and stalk out, slamming the door of the truck as I sit in the passenger seat.

"Whoa." Axel's eyebrows lift as he looks at me.

"Don't ask." I shake my head. "Just get me to a bar."

"Done." He peels out of my house, the tires screeching as they slide on the ice.

"Don't kill us," I bark out, and my hand grips the dashboard.

"Sorry," he shrugs. "Clarke's okay?"

"Yup." I lean my shoulders against the seat, but even the soft leather won't lessen the tension rolling off them.

Once we're seated at the bar, Axel turns to look at me and says, "Okay, tell me what happened."

"Amelia," I growl low enough for only him to hear me.

"Hey!" Ainsley halts when she sees my face. "Sorry, I can come back to take your order when you're ready."

"We're ready," Axel reassures her.

"Sam Adams?" she asks him. "And Johnny Black for you, right? Neat?"

"Yeah, thanks," my chest deflates with a heavy exhale.

"No prob. Be back in a sec." She bounces off to serve our drinks, all the while chatting with customers.

"What did she do now?" Axel's voice rings with annoyance.

"Huh?" I turn my gaze away from Ainsley and look at him. "Oh, she stated I mistreated her." I shake my head and blow out a deep breath.

"Are you fucking kidding me?" Axel slams his hand on the bar. I widen my eyes in warning and clench my jaw. "Sorry," he settles back down on the barstool.

"This is bullshit, though," he whispers.

"I know. There's only one way to end this, and I'm hoping to take care of it tomorrow."

"What are you going to do?" His brows pull together.

"Say the truth," I shrug. Axel was the only person who knew about my relationship with Reese and the reality of my marriage to Amelia. He warned me against it, and he has yet to say he told me so. For that, I'm grateful. I don't need someone else pointing out my mistakes.

"Here you go." Ainsley places our drinks in front of us with a hesitant smile.

"Thanks," I tell her, my smile just as tight.

When she walks away, Axel continues speaking. "I say do what you need to do to clear your name. This is crap, and we both know it. Cheers." He touches his bottle to my glass and takes a healthy pull of his beer.

Saturday night at Clarke's means a larger crowd than I've seen in a long time. Some people come up to talk to me, others keep their distance, their wandering eyes scrutinizing me. I'm sure they've heard the latest gossip. Determined to stand my ground and prove them wrong, I hold my head up high and nod in their direction when I catch them staring.

"I'll be back," Axel steps off his stool and walks toward the crowd. I watch him approach a group of people and tilt my head. He hasn't mentioned he's dating anyone, but I watch him hug a woman with familiarity. Squinting my eyes, I smile. It's Lia Montgomery, Axel's best friend.

Shaking my head, I turn around and face the bar, rolling my empty glass between my fingers.

"Want another round?" Ainsley asks with a smile.

"Why the hell not?" I shrug and place the glass in front of her. I take her in as she serves my whiskey, long blonde hair framing her blue eyes and full lips now pulled between her teeth.

I follow her line of vision. "You have a thing for him?" I lean forward, resting my arms on the counter.

"Hell no. No offense," she laughs. "He's great, but more like a brother. It's hard to make friends when you're new to a small town like this, and Axel didn't hesitate to be friendly."

"He's definitely social. Although, it doesn't seem like you have trouble with the customers." I tilt my head and stare at her.

"Working is one thing, but actually making friends my age is another. Everyone here has known each other since they were kids, so let's just say it hasn't been easy being part of a group of friends." She shrugs as if it didn't matter, but her downcast eyes communicate a different emotion.

"Axel has introduced me to a few people, but besides a quick hello when they come in here to order drinks, they don't take notice of me outside of this bar."

"Well, that's a shame. It's their loss." I lean further across the bar and whisper, "Between you and me, some of these people can be stuck-up." My butt hits the stool again when I hear someone call out her name from the other side of the bar. She smiles gratefully and goes on to do her job, leaving me with my whiskey.

I relate to her. It hasn't been easy being back here for as long as I've been. Usually, I'd visit for a day or two in between commitments, not giving people the chance to ask too many questions. Now, with my impending divorce, the uncertainty of the future of my music career, and all the rumors, the people here haven't hidden their curiosity about my long-term stay.

chapter 3

Knox

I park my truck at the entrance of Grand Teton National Park and hop out, inhaling the fresh air into my lungs. I rub my hands together, grabbing my gloves from the center console inside my truck. I look out at the beauty of the snow-covered mountains and begin walking. I love driving up here, appreciating the changing leaves on the trees and being away from curious glances.

Hopefully, my lawyer will find a way for me to tell the public the truth behind my marriage to Amelia and not get my ass handed to me with a lawsuit from the label. He sounded hopeful this morning when we spoke and promised to look through every detail with immense scrutiny.

I should've taken my time to look into different labels instead of signing with the first one that offered me a deal, but I was young, and RWB Records was one of the top labels every artist wanted to sign with. I scrub my face and sigh. No sense in wishing for a different past when it's already done.

I begin to follow the trail, the light snow covering the ground crunching beneath my boots. This part of the park is empty since I'm probably the only person willing to come here when the weather's cold and the path is snowy.

As I walk, I reflect on my future. Firstly, I need to release my feelings for Reese. I'll never fully move forward if I'm still holding on to her emotionally, stirring the resentment I'm holding against everyone that had a hand in creating this reality, beginning with myself.

At one point, she was everything I ever wanted. She was my whole world until something else became my priority, and that's a mistake I'll never make again. In doing that, I also stopped making myself a priority and my happiness came second the moment I put money first in my life.

I scrub a hand down my face and release a shaky breath. Reese and I are history, from the moment I signed the contract with RWB Records. All that's left now is for me to get my life back on track, one I truly want and not a cut up version someone else creates for me.

Until I let this go, I'll never want to play music again. It will always remind me of what I lost. I also don't want to hurt Reese more than I already have. I'll always love her in some way, but we're over, and the sooner I accept that, the better it will be for everyone.

Shaking the memory of her smile from my mind, I look out onto the lake I'm rounding and pause to take in the beauty around me. I may not be in the best place in my life, but I'm grateful for this kind of peace. Moments like this, away from the drama, make each day bearable. I don't know why I ever agreed to live in Los Angeles when I've always been a country boy at heart. The speed of the city drowns me while this quiet seclusion fuels me.

Maybe I'll even start writing songs again. God, it's been years since I've written a song, but I'll need more than a walk around here to spark that inspiration. I keep on wandering, nowhere close to figuring out my life but definitely feeling calmer.

Once I'm ready to head back into town and warm up, I make my way to my truck. This trip was a waste when it came to making a plan, but at least I got out of the house and visited a place I love. That in itself will help get my mind right again.

Back in town, I stop at the coffee shop, Cup-O-Joe, before heading back home.

"Hey," I hear from a few feet away while I wait for my coffee. I turn to find Ainsley sitting at a table.

"Hi," I respond with a small wave.

"Want to take a seat?" she asks, organizing the papers lying on the table.

"Um... It's okay," I scratch the back of my neck.

"Sorry, I probably shouldn't have asked. Just thought... Never mind." She looks around to check if anyone is watching us. Of course, they are. They always are.

"Sure." I grab my cup and take a seat, feeling like an ass after she mentioned it's been hard for her to make friends.

"You don't have to, really. I'm sure you have things to do and..."

"Ainsley," I stop her from rambling.

"Yeah?" she looks up at me with wide eyes.

"It's okay. I was going to go home because I hate that people are making assumptions about my life," I explain.

"Oh, that makes sense." She nods and leans back in her seat, sipping her coffee.

"Are you working?" I nod to the pile of papers.

"I'm going through mail my grandmother forwarded to me."

"You've been living here for a few months, right?" I ask.

"Yeah. I know, I know, I should have all my mail forwarded to this address, but I wasn't sure how long I'd stay at first. Actually, that's a lie, I'm just a procrastinator."

I laugh at her honesty. "What made you want to move to Everton?"

"Honestly, looking for adventure. After I found out my ex-boyfriend cheated on me, I had nothing holding me back in Denver, so I wanted a change of scenery. It was either go to Texas, where my grandmother lives, or throw a dart at a map and see where destiny led me," she says this as if it were the most normal approach.

"You let a dart choose where you were going to live?" I raise my eyebrows.

"Why the hell not? If I didn't like the place when I arrived, I could just throw another dart. Anyway, Everton was where the dart landed, and here I am, working as a bartender when I've never served drinks before, but it's cool to try something new." She lifts a shoulder, her pink, chipped nails flicking at the corner of one of the envelopes.

Impressed, I say, "Hat's off to you for not letting a cheating bastard bring you down."

"Oh, don't get me wrong, I grabbed his favorite possessions and lit them on fire in the front yard. When he got home that night, his favorite jersey, expensive sneakers, and huntin' rifle were sitting in a burnt pile."

I chuckle. "Remind me not to get on your bad side." I take a drink of my coffee.

"You're safe," she smiles. "Anyway, so I grabbed the mail on the way out to get coffee and figured I'd take a look at it."

"Are you originally from Texas?"

"Yeah, from Dallas. My parents retired recently, and they're traveling the US in a camper, so my grandmother was willing to forward anything that seemed important," she relaxes into the chair as she talks about her family. Her southern drawl makes an appearance as she speaks.

"Well, it seems like the adventurous spirit runs in your family," I mirror her posture, relaxing as well.

"They actually inspired me to make the move. I figured if they could do it in their sixties, I could move somewhere new at thirty-two."

Talking to Ainsley is refreshing. She doesn't act like some star-struck fan, fumbling over her words, or flirting to get in my pants. She's being herself as she tells me about her family and I laugh at her initial reaction of Everton—a picture-perfect town that seemed to belong in a snow globe.

She's quirky and approachable. I don't understand why she hasn't made many friends here. Before I head out, I look at her. "If you want a friend, just let me know. I could use one myself," I offer.

"Thanks, I appreciate that," she nods, smiling wide.

"No problem. I'm gonna go, but I'm sure I'll see you around." I tap the wooden table and stand, walking out of the coffee shop and heading back home, feeling lighter.

♪

I've spent the whole morning thinking about Ainsley's approach to a new beginning. When she shared that with me yesterday, I was impressed. I've never met anyone who took a chance like that. Hell, the last time I closed my eyes and jumped was when I moved to Nashville, everything after that was premeditated and planned to the second.

I've been conditioned to that type of planning and maybe that's the first thing I need to break before I can decide where to go with my life. I need to get rid of the feeling that everything needs to be perfectly arranged.

Feeling useless, I refill my mug and sit at the kitchen counter, reading over my paperwork, focusing on the fine print. Unsure of what to look for, I grab my iPad and start researching for things that will disqualify a non-disclosure agreement.

Every time I find a reason that could invalidate it, I look through the contract in search of that. Eventually, my eyes blur from staring at printed words, and I stand to stretch my body, taking a break. This is why I pay my lawyer well, so I won't have to do his job, but I feel like each day that I sit here doing nothing is a day I could be free from this bullshit.

I rinse my mug and place it in the dishwasher before going down to the gym in my basement and getting lost in a workout.

I ignore the text message notifications that intrude my exercise and keep pushing until my phone rings. Running a towel down my face, I let out a deep sigh and check the screen. I ignore the missed call and a couple of text messages from Harris. My eyes continue to scan the list of messages until one stops me.

Smiling, I open the message from my friend, actor and producer Matthew Barber. We met years ago when I worked on the soundtrack for a movie he was in and became fast friends. It was nice to have someone honest in Los Angeles.

I read over his message and respond. He'll be in Montana for a few days, and he wants to get together. It'll be nice to catch up with him this week and talk to someone who understands how this business works. It seems glamorous from the outside, but only those of us who work in it know the brutal honesty behind being a celebrity.

Happy to have something to look forward to this week, I shower and head to my parents' house, hoping I can get in a ride on my horse. I have yet to ride Ty since I arrived, and a little alone time with my horse is always medicine for the soul.

I say a quick hello to my mom, giving her a peck on her cheek before promising I'll be back in after my ride. I head to Ty's stall and take in his healthy form. His dark brown hair is only interrupted on three of his legs, where he has white sock markings. A smile tugs on my lips when he approaches me, bobbing his head. I reach out and pet him when he becomes familiar with my scent.

"Ready to go on a ride, buddy?" I run my hand down the length of his face before grabbing the saddle.

Climbing on, I steer him out of the barn and begin riding through the property, grateful there are 300 acres for me to roam around. I adjust my black cowboy hat before taking off in a trot. The cold air brushes past me as I let Ty lead the way. He's free to move and take me where he wants. I'm not controlling this, not today.

I stare at the mountains on our property. As a kid, having this much land never made me feel like I lived in a tiny town. I always felt like I had enough space to move around and get away when I needed some time to myself. When it was time to buy my own house, I made sure to choose one that offered the same feeling. I may not have a ranch and acreage, but I have my own sacred space where I can disconnect and have privacy. Amelia hated coming here, which was fine by me since it gave me the opportunity to visit on my own and get away from the mess of our marriage. I just wished I could stay longer than a day or two when I'd stop by here. It was a given that this is where I'd come once I took a step back from the spotlight, but when you're as famous as I am in the music industry, the spotlight never really turns off.

Ty's neigh brings me back to the present, and I look up to see my dad riding toward me.

"Hey," I say when he's close enough to hear me.

"Sneaking out as well?" He smirks.

"Yeah. It's been too long."

"Come on." He tilts his hat-covered head and pulls up beside me, both of our horses taking us in the same direction at a slow pace. "What's on your mind?" he asks.

I shake my head. "Where do I begin? Failure, for one," I confess.

My dad looks at me, his eyebrows pinched together. "No, son, you're not a failure. You went out and fought for your dream. You made a name for yourself, on your own."

I scoff at that. "It wasn't on my own, Dad."

"You can argue with me, but you moved to Nashville and got noticed on your own. You got people interested in you and your music. Not many people can say they've succeeded in that. You're known worldwide, and you've toured in Europe, the US, Canada. Your fans love you. Don't let one bump stop you from doing what you love. It ain't worth it." He shakes his head.

"That's just it, I don't know if I love this anymore. The industry is so twisted and fake. What the fans see is all an illusion. They don't know the real me because I was told how to dress, act, perform."

"Well, then maybe it's time you show them the real you," my dad suggests with a conspiring smirk.

"I need to figure out how to get out of my contract with the label with minimum repercussions." I blow air out between my chapped lips.

"You'll get it done. It's your freedom, and sometimes there's a high price to pay for it. But it's worth it."

"Thanks, Dad. How are things here?" I look out onto the land.

"Great. Can't complain. We're glad you're here for some time, even if under these circumstances. You've been missed."

"I've missed this place, too," I smile, turning to look at him.

"I don't know anything about being famous, but I know a hell of a lot about hard work. Some years are better than others, but giving up is never an option. Had I given up the first year this ranch was unsuccessful, who knows where we'd be right now? You pull through, testing different options until you find the one that works." His words ring through me, meant to encourage me.

If music is in my future, I need to find a way to fit it into my life without me changing everything about myself to fit in it. It was never supposed to be that way.

Harris's suggestion about creating my own label comes to the forefront of my mind. Shaking my head, I get rid of the thought. It isn't that it's impossible, it's that I need to make sure I want a life in the public eye again before taking that route.

My dad and I finish our ride and go into the house. I grab the beer he offers and take a seat in the living room, where Axel joins us. Every so often, my mind wanders to Reese, but I shut it down before I go down a path that I'm no longer allowed to walk.

chapter 4

"Fucking hell, it's freezing here," Matt says, trembling as he makes his way to my truck from the airport.

"Welcome to Wyoming. Montana's the same way," I state.

"I know, but it shocked me. It's good to see you, man." He pats my back in a half-hug.

"You, too." When he called and told me he was flying into Wyoming before driving to Montana, I offered to pick him up and have lunch. "How's Tinley?"

"She's great. She's meeting me in Montana in a couple days."

"Good stuff. It's nice to get away every now and then," I reply.

"Tell me about it. How are you holding up? I read the latest. I'm sorry, buddy." He shakes his head in disbelief.

"If anyone knows how shitty this is, it's you. My only wish is that Amelia would let it be and sign the divorce papers." She would make it much easier if she agreed and granted me the divorce. I know she doesn't love me either, so I don't know why she's letting this drag.

Matt nods, pensive. "Are you really going to leave country music?" He raises his eyebrows as he looks at me. Everyone is curious about the answer to that question.

I chance a glance as I drive toward town and shrug. "I need time. There's other stuff I need to clear before I can decide. I definitely won't be working with RWB Records anymore."

"I get it. I felt the same way a couple years ago."

I nod, knowing what he went through and how hard it was on him. "Anyway, I'm glad you stopped by here. Not much to see in Everton, but we got food and drinks."

"That's all I need," he says, rubbing his hands.

We arrive at Clarke's and take a seat at a table, people staring at us. I shake my head but ignore their curious glances.

"Looks like Everton is surprised to see us," Matt chuckles.

"No shit. Hopefully, they just stare from their seats." I hope no one approaches us. The last thing I want is Matt to be bombarded by fans.

"Hey," I look up to see Ainsley standing by our table, smiling widely. "I'm Ainsley, and I'll be serving you today."

"Lunch shift?" I ask, tilting my head.

"Yeah, we're short-staffed, so I get to work a double shift. Yay me," she shakes her head but doesn't look the least bit annoyed as she holds her smile in place.

"I'm Matt, it's nice to meet you," he reaches his hand out to shake hers.

"Nice to meet you, too. I'm a huge fan. I didn't know you guys were friends," she glances at me.

I shrug. "LA is a small world."

"I can imagine. Anyway, what can I get you to drink?" She holds a small notepad in her hand and a pen in the other, shaking it between her fingers while she waits for our order.

"A Sam Adams for me," I respond.

"I'll have the same," Matt tells her.

He looks at me after she walks away, eyebrows raised. "What's the deal with her?"

My eyebrows furrow. "Nothing, why?"

"You sure?" he grins.

"She's the bartender here, new to town. Only person that hasn't accused me of the rumors they hear in the news," I explain.

"Uh, huh," he nods, a mischievous smile on his face.

"It's not like that," I defend. I'm not ready to be with anyone, let alone in this small town where everyone is watching what I do and with whom. I've done enough damage to people in the past to continue down that road.

"Well, she's pretty and seems nice." He leaves it at that.

Changing the subject, I ask him what he's working on. It's nice to talk to someone about something else besides my current situation. Matt knows how deceiving this career can be and how frustrating it is to talk about it constantly. I'm grateful we can talk about other things, including sports and his recent film, *The First Lights*.

After lunch, I drive him to the car rental. "Thanks for stopping by. It was good to hang out."

"For sure. If you need anything, call me. It may not seem like it right now, but things will get better, I promise. Don't hide, though. That will only give them more reason to believe the rumors." He squeezes my shoulder reassuringly. Grateful for his advice, I thank him.

"We'll talk," he says as he gets out of my truck.

"Yeah. Tell Tinley I say hi," I call out.

"Will do. She's been asking how you're holding up."

"Appreciate it, and drive safely." He nods and walks into the building.

I drive away, tossing around the advice he shared about hiding. I hit call on my phone and let the ringing sound from my car speakers.

"Hello?" My lawyer, David, answers.

"Hey, David, it's Knox. Any news on the NDA? I was reading over it and researching for things that would invalidate it. All they can do is sue me for damages, but besides that, I won't get any real consequence in a courtroom."

"Yeah, that's right. What are you thinking?"

"If we don't find something by tomorrow afternoon, I'm going to risk it. I want a statement drawn up that discloses the details of my marriage to Amelia. I'm tired of hiding behind this," I explain, no longer willing to wait.

"It may bring about a wave of backlash," he warns.

"I know," I exhale. "I'm ready. I'll get shit for agreeing to this, but it's worse to have people thinking I'd cheat or actually mistreat a woman." My fingers tighten around the steering wheel.

"Okay. I'll keep working on this just in case. There must be something. NDAs aren't always tight, and there's usually something that discredits them. Did they tell you about the plan before you signed?" he asks.

"Yeah, my publicist explained everything before I was given the NDA," I answer, hoping we can hold on to that.

"Great. Give me a day, this may be something we can use."

"Thanks, David." I toss my head back against the headrest while I wait for the green light.

"You're welcome. I'll work on this first and then the contract with the label. Once this information comes to light, they'll come after you, and I want to be prepared to handle them."

"I owe you," I tell him and disconnect the call. For the first time in months, I'm starting to see a shimmer of hope in all of this chaos.

♪

After hearing from David this morning, I call Harris.

"Hey, what's going on?" he answers.

"I need you to act as my manager instead of their pawn and negotiate my contract with the label," I demand.

"I *am* your manager," his words ring with annoyance.

"I want out of my contract. I'll perform in the New Year's Eve show in Nashville, but that's it. The current records I created with RWB will remain royalty share, but I'm free from them." I'm firm in my choice.

"Knox, I don't know if they'll accept that," he's hesitant.

"It's either that, or I share on my social media accounts that my marriage to Amelia was a sham, a stunt the label and our publicists organized to manipulate fans."

"Fuck," his breath sounds through the speaker. "You signed an NDA."

"Harris, you and I both know I was forced to agree to that if I wanted a deal with them. I'm sure the last thing the label wants is for the truth to come out. They won't be happy if people know the extreme manipulation they use on their artists." I change my direction in approaching this situation. If I can get out of my contract sooner than planned, I'll keep the stunt to myself. Right now, I just want to be free to move forward in my life.

"I'll try it. You know I want what's best for you, not just as your manager but as your friend."

I sigh. "I know that. Thanks. If you need anything, call David. He's up to date with everything."

"I will. I'll do my best, but Knox …" he pauses.

"Yeah?"

"Think about staying in the industry under different circumstances. We can create a label and make the music you were meant to." His voice amps up with hope.

"I won't make any promises. Right now, I want to put all of this behind me." I don't want to give him false hope by saying I'll think about it. If I go back to country music, that will probably be the route I take, but right now I need to work on clearing my name and my affiliation to RWB Records.

After hanging up with him, I call David and tell him this plan may just work. I was hesitant at first when he mentioned staying loyal to the NDA and only breaching it if the label didn't grant me what I want. Blackmail at its finest, but it's worth a shot. After all, I'm feeding them their same medicine.

As much as I want to tell everyone the truth about all this, David put things into perspective. I gain nothing by speaking the truth if it pisses the label off and I need to cut ties with them first.

Exhaling, I grab my coat and head to the grocery store. Lord knows I need to stock up my kitchen.

As I'm strolling through the aisles with a cart, I see a familiar face.

"Hey." I walk up to Ainsley.

"Hi." She looks at me with a smile. "Fancy meeting you here." She does a half-curtsey thing that causes me to laugh.

Does this woman ever frown?

"In desperate need of stocking up my kitchen, or I'll be eating at Clarke's every day," I explain.

"Our food's not bad." She shakes her head. "Sure, it's not the healthiest," she shrugs.

"Yup, and sometimes I just want a home-cooked meal."

"You cook?" She raises her eyebrows, her eyes widening almost comically.

I chuckle, "Yeah, don't seem so surprised." I nudge her with my elbow.

"Sorry, just didn't think famous people actually cooked."

"I was a small-town boy before I became famous. If I didn't help out 'round the house, I wouldn't be allowed to play my guitar, so I helped my mom in the kitchen," I share, nostalgia sweeping through me.

"That's cool. I agree nothing beats a home-cooked meal." She lifts her basket.

I look at the contents and furrow my brows. "Fritos and canned chili aren't exactly home-cooked."

"No, but I don't have time to make chili from scratch before work, and I'm craving Frito pie."

"Frito what?" My face screws in confusion.

"Frito pie, you know?" She lifts her basket higher.

"No, I don't." I shake my head.

"You make chili then serve it over Fritos and add cheese and sour cream. God, it's *so* good." She practically moans.

"Never heard of it," I state, shrugging.

"That's insane!" She slaps my forearm. "Oh, sorry." She takes a step back, pursing her lips.

"It's okay. I guess I'm going to have to try this Frito pie thing sometime. It was good to see you." I make my way down the aisle but stop when she calls out to me.

"Want to try it today? I'll have enough for two people. Actually, it'd probably be good that I share if not I'll risk eating it all and I can't afford to do that," she rambles like the day I saw her at the coffee shop.

"Um," I look around the aisle.

"No pressure. I probably shouldn't have asked. Sorry." She turns around to walk away.

"Wait," I call to her. "Why the hell not? Easier than cooking for one. Let me grab a few things before we go?" I ask, just in case she's in a hurry since she works tonight.

"Sounds good, I still need to pick up some stuff, too."

"I'll buy whatever else you need for the Frito pie," I offer.

"No way, I was buying the ingredients anyway."

"Yeah, but instead of having leftovers, or stuffing yourself," I smirk, "you'll have to share with me."

"Ha ha, make fun of me now, but we'll see who asks for seconds later," she mocks, pointing at me as the basket hangs from her arm.

"In that case," I grab a second can of chili. "We'll probably need two of these." I hold it up and shake it.

Her smile lights up her face, her blue eyes shining as her head bobs up and down rapidly. I shake my head and grab what I need before meeting her by the register.

"You can follow me, we're not far from my apartment," she says as she loads her bags into her backseat.

"Sounds good." I walk to my truck and follow her out of the parking lot, questioning what the fuck I'm doing by agreeing to have lunch with her, but her happiness is contagious.

I follow her into her apartment, looking around at the small space. Photographs are sprinkled throughout the room, hanging on the walls and placed on a shelf with some books.

"Is this your grandmother?" I hold up a frame of Ainsley with an older woman.

"That's my Geema," she smiles proudly.

"Cute nickname," I tease, placing the frame back in its place.

"I thought I was cool growing up, making it sound like a rapper's name or something, you know, G-Money, but instead Geema stuck," she giggles. "I'm such a dork." She covers her face with her hand and looks away, unpacking her groceries.

I smile at her and ask, "What can I help you with?" I walk into her narrow kitchen and look around.

"I've got this, you can take a seat and relax."

"No way, you bought the food, so I'll help. Besides, how else will I learn to make Frito pie if I don't help?" I cross my arms.

"True. Okay, it's super easy since we're using canned chili. All we have to do is warm up the chili in a pot. Then, we'll put Fritos in a bowl, pour the chili over it, and top it with cheese and sour cream. It's really a no-brainer." She grabs a pot and puts it over the stove while I open the two cans of chili and pour them inside.

While Ainsley stirs the chili, I divide the Fritos into two bowls. "Is that enough?" I show her one of the bowls.

"A little more. Don't be shy with the Fritos. Carbs are our friend, I promise," her eyes twinkle with a smile.

I laugh and nod. "Okay, so a lot more Fritos." I fill the bowls to her liking and wait for the chili to heat through.

"Do you want something to drink? I should've offered when we first arrived. Not using my best bartending manners at home." She reaches for two glasses. "I've got water, coke, and beer."

"Water is perfect."

She fills the glasses with water from the dispenser on the fridge and hands one to me. "Thanks." I take a chug. "Are you adjusting better to meeting people here?" I ask her.

"Kinda. Working the bar at Clarke's helps some, but I still haven't broken into the cliques of women my age."

"Don't stress it. If they're not willing to get to know you, then it's their loss."

"I guess, but… I don't know. I want to do more than work, and it's kinda awkward to go out by yourself," she frowns.

"Only if you make it awkward. Besides, with time, you'll become more familiar with the locals," I reassure her.

She nods and claps her hands. "Okay, this is done! Moment of truth." She shakes her shoulders in a shimmy, and I stare at her in equal parts amusement and admiration for her constant positive attitude.

She ladles two healthy servings of chili over the Fritos and hands me the shredded cheese. I add some on top of mine and wait for her to finish hers before taking a seat at the small, round table she has in the living room next to the kitchen.

I take a bite and find Ainsley staring with lifted eyebrows, waiting for my assessment. "So?" she taps her fingers together in front of her chest.

"Good thing I grabbed that second can. This is like Fritos nachos."

"Yes," she squeals and dances in her seat before digging in.

I get to know Ainsley a little better as we eat. She asks me about growing up in Everton and is careful to steer clear from any mention of my music career, for which I'm grateful.

"Ugh," Ainsley pushes her empty bowl away from her and pats her stomach. "Two full bowls was way too much."

"And yet you ate it all," I stare at her bowl. She ate as much as I did.

"Hell yeah. I wasn't going to let it go to waste. Thank God I'll be running around the bar all night."

"What time do you have to go in?" Spending the afternoon with her has been nice. It feels good to hang out with someone who isn't fishing for information or treating me like I might explode at any moment.

She cranes her neck to the side and looks at the clock on the oven. "Oh crap," she leaps from her seat and grabs our plates. "I gotta leave in ten."

"I can clean up while you get ready," I offer.

"Will you? Oh my God, thanks," she hugs me and runs to her bedroom. I stand in her apartment, stiff and unsure, before shaking off the feeling and washing the plates and the pot.

"You didn't have to wash them. You could've let them sit in water, and I'd get to it later tonight," she walks out of her room dressed for work in her black slacks and white Clarke's polo.

"You cooked, so it's the least I could do for feeding me," I shrug. "Besides, I doubt you'll want to clean when you get home from work."

"Thanks." She grabs her purse. "Ready?"

I nod and follow her out. "Thanks for lunch. It was better than going home and getting stuck in my thoughts."

"Anytime. It was nice to have company as well. I'll see you around." She hops into her car, her permanent smile causing me to smile in return. I wave before climbing into my truck.

This woman is something else. The more I get to know her, the more Matt's words about opening up pop into my head. I think about Reese, what I put her through, and how painful it was to lose her.

I don't deserve to be happy again.

chapter 5

Knox

"Hello?" I pause my workout as I answer my phone.

"Hey, Knox," David's voice moves through the speaker.

"What's going on?" I sling the towel I was using to wipe my face over my shoulder.

"I've got some updates from Amelia's lawyer. She's refusing to agree to the amount you've offered, despite your marriage being so short that the alimony would only last two years. In other words, she's being difficult on purpose," he states, sounding as annoyed as I feel.

"God, I'm going to have to talk to her. I don't understand why she's acting this way when she doesn't care about me." I run a hand down my face.

"You know I don't advise that. What we can do is set up a meeting, both lawyers present, and see if we can settle on something. If not, we'll have to go to court."

I take a seat on the bench against the wall of my gym and grip the phone. I wanted to avoid going to court and making more of a scandal than necessary, but this is getting out of hand. More of the lies Amelia's spreading continue to get twisted in magazines and online sites.

"Do you think a meeting will help?" I ask, blowing a heavy breath.

"It could. At this point, what do you have to lose?" I can imagine him shrugging as he sits back in his big California office with the Hollywood sign visible from his floor to ceiling windows.

"You're right. Listen, about the rumors she's spreading, can we use that to our advantage?" I stand and begin pacing.

"It would be her word against yours."

"Fine. Set up a meeting and I'll fly out for it," I say with finality. I want this done and over with.

"I'll get back to you. Have you heard from Harris?"

"Not yet, I'm hoping to hear from him today. Two days is enough time for the label to make a decision. If not, they can sue me. I'm done being their puppet." I grind my teeth.

"Let me know. I'll call Amelia's lawyer and get back to you with a date."

I thank him and hang up, cutting my workout short and jumping in the shower. This seems like a never-ending nightmare, but there has to be an end to this madness soon. If I can knock some sense into Amelia, it will help. She's always been insecure despite her success, and I'm assuming her hesitation is due to her belief that without our marriage, she won't be good enough for the public eye. Seeing her in person might soften her attitude.

I head into town and spend some time walking around with no real direction. I don't allow the stares to create a wedge between me and my love for this place. They're just curious, wondering what's true and what isn't. They're probably questioning how much I've changed to live the life they're reading about in the media, and if the boy they knew is the same man standing before them today.

My approach has always been to ignore the rumors and not feed into them. The more I speak up, the more fuel I'll feed the gossip mags. However, with Amelia's recent actions, I may need to release a statement.

If I could turn back time…

I shake that thought away. There's no turning back, there never is, only living the present with the consequences of our actions and learning from them.

"Hey." I turn my head to the right to see Eli standing on the sidewalk.

"What's up?" I shake his hand.

"Grabbing some feed." He juts his head toward Cowboy's Feed Store. "How about you?"

"Taking a walk. I've missed this place, and it isn't exactly easy to get out and walk around without getting some kind of questions thrown my way, but today I said fuck it." I shrug, hooking my thumbs into my jean pockets.

"I can't imagine," he shakes his head. "You sure you're okay?" He narrows his eyes, analyzing me.

"As okay as I can be." I offer a tight smile.

"Let's grab a drink tonight. Clarke's at seven?" he asks.

"Sure." I have to submerge myself back into society at some point.

"Cool. See ya later." He waves over his shoulder and heads into the store.

I keep on walking around the town center, saying hello to the few people who greet me. I'm starting to lose my patience with all of this free time, and I know it's on me to change my routine. Maybe if I try to write something, I'll find my groove again. I've sold millions of records in my career, putting me on top of the industry. There's no reason why I can't keep doing that on my own terms.

I toss the idea around as I head into a diner for lunch before calling Harris for an update.

♪

"You better have good fuckin' news after ignoring my calls all afternoon," I growl, as I answer the call through my car's Bluetooth speaker.

"I was in meetings all day, but I do have good news."

I pause and wait for him to continue. "The label doesn't want the stunt to be made public. It was hard to convince them, which is why I couldn't answer before."

"Stop talking in circles and tell me what they said," I bark out, slamming on my brakes to avoid taking a red light.

"They'll end the contract early, but every term on projects you worked on with them remains the same. That means you'll still have shared royalties for the songs you recorded through them, but you'll be free to do whatever you want in the future as long as you stick to your NDA."

"I can do that," I breathe out. *Finally*.

"One more thing," he pauses. I should've known it wouldn't be this easy. "You must perform on New Year's Eve in Nashville, and you can't damage their reputation by talking about anything that happened."

"Got it, I'll keep quiet. I just want to break away from them." These are the terms I mentioned to Harris when I told him to negotiate for me, so I'm taking this as the first sign of good things coming my way.

"Oh, also," I hear papers rustling on the line. "If you were to decide to start your own label, you can't steal any of their artists," Harris finishes off.

"Did you tell them you suggested that to me?" I ask, pulling into the parking lot in front of Clarke's.

"Hell, no. The label knows I'm your manager, and I work for you, but they didn't ask about any of that. Artists tend to break away and go on their own, so they add that clause," he explains.

"All right. Thanks. Can you call David?"

"I plan to call him now, but I wanted to talk to you first and make sure you agreed with this." Harris's tired voice comes through my speakers. Lately, I've forgotten he was my friend before my manager, and I know I've shut him out.

"I appreciate it. And, Harris," I hesitate. "Whatever I decide, you'll be the first to know." I owe him that. He's been my manager since I started this crazy ride and my friend for longer. He's fought alongside me; I won't leave him in the dark. Even if I am frustrated with my career, he deserves to know what I decide.

"Thanks. If you need anything, call," Harris offers.

"Will do. Gotta go." I hang up and take a few deep breaths, watching the icy rain land on my windshield.

Things took a different path than I planned, but this will guarantee that I can leave RWB Records and start new, whatever I choose to do with my life. Soon, I'll be a free man.

Feeling lighter, I run into Clarke's and sit at the bar while I wait for Eli.

"Look what the rain dragged in," a cheery voice says.

I look up to see Ainsley leaning against the bar, opposite where I'm sitting, her arms crossed against her chest.

"Hey."

"What can I get you? Beer or whiskey?" She tilts her head and uncrosses her arms, letting them fall to her sides.

"Whiskey," I confirm.

She nods and turns to grab a glass and the bottle before she serves the drink in front of me.

"How've you been?" she asks after she's placed the bottle back on the shelf.

"Good, and you?" I take a sip, allowing the amber liquid to warm me up.

"Good. Have you made Frito pie yet?" her eyes light up.

Shaking my head, I chuckle. "Not yet. It's only been two days since I tried it."

"I could eat it every day," she sighs. "It's good to see you genuinely smile," her comment catches me off guard. "When I first met you, you were so grouchy, I almost believed the rumors about you."

"Okay…" I look down at my glass. I've smiled before.

"Don't get me wrong, I can't even imagine what it must be like to be you, and maybe I'd be too serious as well, but it's good to see you lighten up," she repeats.

"Thanks, I think." I take a drink to keep myself busy.

"Sorry if I insulted you." Ainsley reaches out and places her hand on mine. She pulls her hand away quickly when I flinch and looks away, the warmth of her hand imprinted on my skin. I look at her as she works, becoming more curious about her.

"Hey," I call out. I'm about to speak when she turns around, but Eli interrupts me.

"You got here early," he slaps my back and takes a seat next to me, ending the conversation between us before it even got started. Ainsley plasters a smile on her face and greets him, taking his order.

"Cheers," Eli says, knocking his glass to mine. I mimic him and drink my whiskey, wondering what's going on through Ainsley's mind.

I don't mention anything about the label when Eli asks, wanting to be sure about my future before announcing it. I'd like to be the one to share the news with the public when the time comes, and not have it spread around town.

When Eli goes to the bathroom, I lean over the bar and get Ainsley's attention. "Sorry about earlier. It just took me by surprise."

"It's okay, really. It's nothing," she shakes her head, preparing a Jack and Coke while we talk.

"It's not. I'm just…" How do I say this without sounding presumptuous?

"Honestly, Knox, it's no big deal," she brushes me off, making her way to serve the drink she was making.

"It's…"

"Hey, Bentley, you've got your own women to entertain. Leave this one to us," Old McFord, another rancher in town, calls out, adjusting his cowboy hat. His words slur slightly.

"Yeah, man, you've got a hot wife and that side candy. Don't be greedy. Us town folk can't get those California women, so leave this one for us," Jim, McFord's brother, agrees.

My jaw clenches. "What did you say?" I stalk over to them, knocking him back on his stool.

"Hey," McFord places his hand on my chest to push me away. I look down at his hand before ripping it away from my body.

"Y'all have no idea what you're talkin' about, and that's no way to treat a lady. Your momma must be turning in her grave, hearing the way you're talking about Ainsley. Show some respect." My nostrils flare.

"We're just sayin' what everyone's read about ya," McFord shrugs as if my fist isn't about to slam into his face.

"Ain't you ever learn you can't believe everything you read?" I get in his face, my body shaking and fists ready to punch him.

"What the hell?" Eli pulls me away, holding me back as he stands between the two older men I'd like to punch manners into and me.

"Get your friend under control," Jim warns.

"Or what?" I yell.

"You know we don't tolerate violence in this town," he says.

I shake my head and look at Ainsley, her eyes wide and hand covering her mouth. She deserves better than this.

I take a step back and look around the bar. "Anyone else have something to say to my face?" I hold my arms open. "Stop being cowards and say it. I can't believe y'all would believe that shit instead of the person you've known your entire lives. So much for being 'one of us'," I use air quotes for emphasis. "I'm only one of you when it's convenient for Everton to have a resident celebrity."

"Come on," Eli pushes me back and toward our spot at the bar.

Anger rolls down my body, and I can't shake it off. "You okay?" I ask Ainsley.

"Yeah, thanks." She looks away.

I scratch my beard and breathe away my anger. When Eli asks what happened, I shake my head and remain silent. Reacting to two old ranchers isn't what I needed to do, but I couldn't stay quiet when they were disrespecting a woman and insulting me. I lift my glass toward Ainsley and chug the whiskey as it burns down my throat.

"Gotta go," I slam down a fifty for both of our drinks and walk out of Clarke's without a backward glance.

chapter 6

Knox

The last few days have been filled with phone calls from both David and Harris, scheduling meetings, and booking a last-minute flight to Los Angeles in the hopes that I can kill two birds with one stone—getting a divorce and breaking my contract—before I leave the city. This chaos needs to end.

I stop at the grocery store to grab a pack of Buffalo Jerky for Harris. He loves that stuff, and I owe him for fighting on my behalf.

"Is this our new meeting place?"

I turn around to find Ainsley, hands on her hips, and a crooked grin on her face. Her long, blonde hair is tied high in a ponytail, showing off the curve of her neck.

"I guess so," I take her in, tight jeans and a long-sleeved tee that fits her just right. Fuck. I squeeze my eyes shut and shake away my thoughts.

"Jerky?" She's standing in front of me now, grabbing the pack from my hand as she reads it.

"It's for my manager. He loves this stuff, and I wanted to take him some as thanks and peace offering. Let's just say I haven't exactly been kind to him lately," I explain.

"Grouchy Knox being unkind?" she teases, her eyes opened wide in mock disbelief.

"Give me that," I yank the jerky from her, playfully.

She giggles and pats my arm. "I'm only kidding."

"I know," I crack a smile. "I gotta go, though, if I don't want to miss my flight."

"Oh, you're going to Nashville?" she asks.

"LA," I correct her.

"Cool. Good luck," she offers a tight smile, all teasing gone.

"Thanks. I'm definitely gonna need it, so I'll take all the luck you want to send my way." If I could have just a hint of her positivity and enthusiasm, this trip would be a breeze. Since I've met her, her happiness has started to seep into me slowly, giving me hope.

"I'll send it all your way," she states with a firm nod. "Now, go on before you miss your flight, and you're stuck at Clarke's tonight with me servin' your drinks." I smile at the vision of her teasing me behind the bar. I'd much prefer to spend the night with her. *Whoa.*

I thank her and pay, reminding myself that I do more damage than good to the women in my life.

"It's about time you arrived," Harris, my manager, says as he meets me outside the airport.

"Fucking weather delay." My good mood from earlier left long ago when I had a two-hour delay in Wyoming.

"David is waiting for you. We'll go see him first, so we don't keep Her Majesty waiting any longer." Harris rolls his eyes. He never was a fan of Amelia.

"I just hope she signs the papers. I'm giving her the house, alimony, and peace. I don't know what else she wants." I shake my head, stripping out of my jacket and tossing it in the backseat of his car. "It's hot as hell," I roll up the sleeves of my sweater.

"Welcome to LA," Harris grins.

"Sure as hell haven't missed it," I sigh and lock my seatbelt. "Let's get this over with."

Harris speeds down the highway and toward downtown Los Angeles, swerving between cars with a precision only he has. I grip the handle the entire time, hoping we make it in one piece.

"Wish me luck," I tell Harris when he pulls up to David's office building.

"It'll be okay. I'll see you at the label when you're done."

"Thanks," I leave my bags in his car and stalk to the building, taking the elevator to the eighteenth floor.

"Knox," I turn to see David, worry lines around his eyes.

"Sorry. I got here as fast as I could." I shake his hand as I explain. I kept him updated about my flight, but I know being late isn't exactly the most ideal situation.

"I know. Come on." I follow him into a conference room where Amelia and her lawyer are sitting.

"It's about damn time."

"Nice to see you as well, Amelia," I smirk to hide my disdain.

She rolls her eyes and looks at her lawyer. "Do you hear his sarcasm?"

"Don't start. You're the one with the attitude. I just want to sign the papers and be done." I take a seat across from her.

"I don't agree with your terms." She leans back and crosses her arms, a perfect arch to her brow.

"What else do you want? I'm giving you the house for *free*, great alimony for the timespan required by the state of California, and you'll still receive royalty payments for the songs you were featured in." I have no idea what else she could want.

I take a deep breath to calm myself. "Amelia, we both know our marriage was never based on love, so don't try to throw that out there. No one in this room would buy it. It served a purpose, and now we're done. You're so loved by your fans, this divorce would probably add to your fame. That's what you want, right? Not to fade into the background." I'm hanging on to anything I can to convince her. Truth is, she's a talented singer and has a huge following, she doesn't need me.

"All I ask is that you stop spreading lies. You and I both know I treated you with the utmost respect, and insinuating that I was abusive in any form is bullshit. That's not going to help you get what you want, because I will come out and say the truth," I raise my eyebrows.

She sits up straighter and flares her nostrils. "What truth?" Her words are defensive.

I shrug. "Take back what you said and this all ends. You keep your reputation, and we both move on. However, if you want to play dirty, it won't do you any good."

"I have no idea what you're talking about," she clasps her hands together, resting them on the dark, oak table.

"CJ," is all I say and observe as understanding dawns on her face. I give her a cocky grin and lean back in my seat, stretching my legs out under the table and feeling more relaxed. I wasn't going to bring this up, but I'll give back just as good.

"I have no idea what you're talking about." She knows damn well I know who he is.

"Our house has a security system. Cameras everywhere that are turned on when neither of us are supposed to be home," I arch a brow.

Her face blanches. "No," she lets out on a whisper.

"Yes. We were both supposed to be away for appearances that weekend. I don't care who you fucked while we were married, but I doubt your fans would feel the same way," I threaten, and I hate taking this route.

"You're lying," she continues to fight me.

"David," I look at my lawyer.

"He's seen it?" She shoots up on her seat, back ramrod straight.

"I thought I was lying?" I tilt my head. I have her right where I want her. Amelia cares too much about what others think about her.

Her lawyer looks at her with a stern look and Amelia sits back down.

"No one else has seen the footage, but he had it saved for me so it wouldn't land in the wrong hands," I explain, feeling a tiny bit of compassion for her.

I knew she wasn't loyal to me, and I didn't expect her to be. I took from her physically what I needed when I needed it because it was easier to fuck my wife than have to deal with the cheating accusations. When she finally told me about CJ, I ended our physical relationship and filed for divorce so we could both be happy, which is why I don't understand her reluctance.

"Listen, we can both be happy if we just sign today. I'm asking you as a friend and the person who has lived with you for the past four years. Let's put this behind us." I lean forward, praying she agrees.

"You wouldn't publicize that video," she continues to fight me.

I exhale and shake my head, tired of her crap. "Don't push me, Amelia," I say with finality and stand. "You have three hours to decide. You're already aware of the consequences." I stand and walk out of the room without looking back. It's time I take my life in my own hands.

I shoot David a message letting him know I'm going to the label and will be back to hear her decision and take action if necessary.

If there's one thing I've learned about being a celebrity, it's that you have to play dirty with dirty.

Calling a car service, I wait outside of the building. When the black Town Car pulls up in front of me, I climb in and ask him to take me to RWB Record's Los Angeles office.

♪

"At least this is done," Harris says, shaking my hand as we stand on the sidewalk in front of RWB Record's building.

"Thanks," I nod. "I appreciate what you did." The executives at RWB Records weren't as easy as I was hoping, expressing they want to make the official announcement about our separation, saying it was based on artistic differences. At this point, I'm okay with that. Nothing will ever seem real in this industry regardless of who makes the announcement.

"Where are you staying?" Harris asks.

"Airport hotel. I'm leaving early tomorrow."

"Want to grab dinner?" He leans against his car, parked on the street.

"I almost forgot." I open the back door and pull out my backpack, grabbing the jerky and tossing it to him.

He catches it and smiles. "Thanks, man." He tears open the plastic packet and grabs a piece. "I'm going to have to visit you more often to stock up on these things." Harris would travel between Los Angeles and Nashville with me, finally settling down in Los Angeles when I made it my permanent home.

"You're welcome anytime. I'll let you know about dinner. I want to check in with David first." I haven't heard from him, but I hope he has good news when I get to his office.

"I'll drive you over and wait, so I can drop you off at the hotel."

"Thanks." I take him up on his offer and let David know I'm on my way. If I have to wait for a car, I'll never get to his office on time.

Once I'm up on his floor, David's waiting for me again by the receptionist's desk.

"So?" I ask as he leads me to the conference room we used earlier.

"She agreed," he smiles and pats my back.

"Thank fuck." I stare up at the ceiling and close my eyes, rubbing my eyes with my fingers.

"I know you didn't want to hit her with the threats, but it worked. Her reputation is more important than your marriage," David shrugs.

"I was hoping it would work because I didn't want to make that public, and she would've known I was bluffing." I put my hands in my pocket and look at the papers sitting on the table.

"Ready to sign?" He holds up a pen.

"Hell yes." I grab the pen and sign to end my marriage, grateful this trip wasn't a waste.

I thank David when I'm done and walk out into the late afternoon, feeling free for the first time in years. I stare up the sky and send a quick thanks to the Man upstairs. Memories of Reese hit me, and I blow out a guilty breath. All I can hope is that she's happy. It's all I've ever wanted for her.

I run a hand down my cheeks, tugging my beard at my chin.

"So?" Harris asks.

I nod. "She signed," I confirm.

"Congrats," he grabs my hand and pats my back in a half-hug. "What now?" He looks at me with a question he's been holding in.

"I'm gonna go to the hotel, shower, and celebrate with dinner and drinks. You down?"

"Fuck yeah," he cheers.

"After that, I need to decide what I want to do with my career, but I'll keep you in the loop. If it's music, I'd love for you to continue being my manager, but I need some time to take in every option," I explain, wanting to be fully honest with him.

"Sounds good," he nods.

Ready to shower and eat something, we head to the hotel and make plans to meet in two hours at a nearby restaurant.

chapter 7

Knox

I got to Everton yesterday and drove straight to my parents' house to share the news with them. We celebrated with whiskey and my mom's famous chili, which reminded me of Ainsley. I accepted the leftovers my mom offered, hoping I can make Frito pie for Ainsley.

She's somehow snuck into my mind with her carefree attitude and gentle spirit. I find myself wanting to spend more time with her and get to know her more. She's sparked light into my life in the short time I've known her.

I walk into Clarke's, sure that Ainsley will be working the bar, and take a seat.

"What can I get ya?" Adam barks.

"Whiskey," I reply as I look around the place for Ainsley.

He doesn't reply as he serves my drink and slides it toward me, walking to another customer demanding his attention. Maybe Ainsley is running late, which would explain Adam's attitude. Either that or the guy can't stand me.

I take a sip, setting my feet on the stool rung and relax for the first time in months. The stress of the divorce and my music label have taken a toll on me, but now I can make any decision I want without worrying about NDAs, marriage certificates, or music contracts.

RWB Records hasn't made an announcement yet, but I've prepared my own press release once they do. As for the divorce, Amelia and I both agreed to share an exclusive statement with Music & Life Magazine this weekend.

There's been a lot of speculation about the future of my career, and it will only increase with the upcoming news, so I'm bracing myself for the questions that will be thrown my way.

Checking the time, I ask Adam if Ainsley works tonight.

"She's sick," he calls out as he takes an order.

Damn.

Before I can change my mind, I pay for my drink and leave Clarke's, heading home to grab the chili my mom made yesterday. On my way to Ainsley's house, I stop at the grocery store and buy Fritos and cheese.

"Hello?" a mussed, blanket-wrapped Ainsley answers the door. "What are you doing here?" Her eyes are slits as she peeks up at me.

"Heard you were sick and I brought some comfort food." I hold up the bag and container.

"You didn't have to." She shakes her head, looking down at herself. All I see is the blanket burrito she's wrapped in.

"I wanted to," I smirk and wait for her to let me in.

"Thanks." She sneezes as she opens the door wider.

"Bless you. Now, take a seat while I prep this." I walk straight into her kitchen and get to heating up the chili.

"Did you make chili?" she hovers over me.

"My mom did, and I thought it'd be perfect for some Frito pie. I went to Clarke's, but Adam told me you were sick, so here I am." I open my arms wide, motioning around her apartment.

"Thanks." She sits at the table. "How was LA?"

I peer over my shoulder at her. "Great," I smile with a nod.

"I'll take it everything worked out?" She wipes her red nose with a wrinkled tissue.

"Yeah. It will be shared officially soon, but I was able to end my contract with the label, keeping only the New Year's Eve show I had planned."

"That's awesome. Congrats! Although, it's kind of odd to congratulate an artist for no longer having a record deal," she chuckles, which causes her to sneeze.

"What can I say? I'm here to keep things interesting," I smirk.

"That you are," her words are a whisper, but I pick up on them. I glance her way quickly and catch a blush as she pretends to cough into her blanket. She's definitely not an actress.

"Okay, ready for Frito pie?" I ask her, placing two bowls on the table.

"I'm always ready for Frito pie." She takes a bite and moans. "Oh man, this chili beats canned chili any day of the week. It's almost as good as my Geema's." Her eyes sparkle.

"Glad you like it." One side of my lip tilts up in a smile as I watch her devour the next bite.

We eat in silence for a few minutes before she speaks up again. "Thanks for bringing this. I'll confess I was starving and didn't have the energy to make anything."

"You're welcome. Figured it was the least I could do." I'm not sure why I feel like I owe her something, or maybe it's just an excuse to see her.

"Well, I appreciate it." She sighs and leans back, the blanket having dropped around her waist while she ate, making it obvious she isn't wearing a bra under her sweater. I clear my throat and shift in my seat as I take a long drink of water.

I'm not blind to Ainsley's natural beauty, even sick with a cold, but it wouldn't be fair to her. I need to be fully over Reese and my mistakes before I let a woman into my life. Even if she's funny, gorgeous, and carries herself with confidence.

"Do you want more?" I offer.

"No, thanks." She covers herself with the blanket again as I clear the table and wash the dishes. I quickly adjust myself before turning back toward her.

"Want to watch a movie?" she smiles, hopeful.

"Sure." I sit on the couch next to her, a need to take care of her filling me. I shake it off, questioning what the hell is going on with me.

Without asking, she puts on a movie and leans back into the couch as a Christmas movie begins to play on the television. A content sigh escapes her lips as a soft smile forms on her face. She looks peaceful.

"I love cheesy Christmas movies," she turns to look at me. "I know they're totally predictable, but they're so romantic." Her body relaxes and moves closer to me on her exhale.

I remain quiet as the movie plays, not paying attention to it. Instead, I'm wondering what it is this woman is making me feel. Hope, for starters. It's been a long time since I've felt hopeful about my life, and it's been even longer since I felt like I could care about another woman who wasn't Reese, but this funny and courageous woman is changing my belief.

I look to my left when I feel a thud on my shoulder. Holding in my laughter, I move Ainsley's sleeping body a bit, so her head can rest comfortably on my shoulder, and I wrap an arm around her body. Her warmth surrounds me, and I tighten my arm around her.

I lean my head back on the sofa and close my eyes. Pressure builds in my chest as I hold her, wanting more than this. I also want to hold her when she's awake, when she's aware of my arms around her body.

I push back loose strands of hair from her face and take in her peaceful, sleeping face. Her breath is soft, her lips parted, tempting me to kiss her. She's peace wrapped in a body, and I've been soaking her up, every last drop.

I lick my dry lips and clear my throat as I reach for the remote to lower the volume. Ainsley shifts next to me and squints her eyes open.

"Sorry," her voice is hoarse as she sits up and stretches her arms over her head, exposing her hard nipples through her sweater.

Fuck. My dick notices, too, wanting to make itself present.

I clear my throat. "It's okay. Why don't you get some rest so you can feel better tomorrow?"

She nods as she blinks her eyes open. "Thanks." Her eyes bore into mine, holding me captive with her gaze.

"Anytime." I reach out, cupping her cheek and running my thumb over her soft skin. I lean forward and kiss her forehead, her breath catching in her throat. "Feel better," I whisper as I stand from the couch.

She follows me to the door, watching me step into the elevator before locking up behind her.

As I drive home, I think of the possibility of falling for another person. For so many years, I didn't have that freedom, and I imagine what it would be like.

Would I want to expose that person to the challenges that come with my name and career? It's why I decided to keep my relationship with Reese a secret and look at how that turned out. I won't do that again. The next woman I make a part of my life will not be a secret. It would have to be her choice to be with someone like me, a celebrity who can't exactly hide and expect to have privacy. It's a rare chance I get complete solitude, even in this small town.

I rub the back of my neck as I breathe heavily. I don't even know if Ainsley would want anything to do with me romantically, but I can't be the only one that feels the chemistry between us.

Ainsley may just be the woman who makes me believe in second chances.

chapter 8

Ainsley

I stretch my body in bed, yawning widely and kicking off the heavy blanket. As I rub my eyes, I smile. Knox came over yesterday and brought comfort food. I touch my forehead, where the memory of his kiss is imprinted. I push my head against the pillow and squeeze my eyes shut, but that doesn't stop my smile from growing.

As much as my crush on him has been growing, his life is complicated. Besides, he's a famous musician. There's no way someone like him will stay in a town like this for long, even if it is his home, especially for a woman like me who moved on a whim, working a job with no real future.

My smile turns into a frown.

Sometimes I shake my own head at my crazy idea, but I don't regret it one bit. Moving here was the best adventure, even if it has been challenging immersing myself into the town camaraderie.

Knox is one of the few who has been genuinely kind. I'm not an idiot, I know most of the men that have been nice to me have ulterior motives. I may seem young, but I've got enough life experience to know the difference between authentic friendship and someone looking out for themselves.

Feeling better after a full night's rest, I get out of bed and make coffee before finding my phone sitting on the table in front of the couch. I plop on the worn cushions and take a sip of my coffee while scrolling through my Instagram feed. I can't resist the temptation, so I check Knox's account and see that most of his posts are tour dates, short music teasers, and concert photos. I'm guessing he isn't the one who manages that account, but a girl can wish that he'd suddenly post a photo of himself she can daydream about.

My eyebrows furrow as I click on the newest post and zoom in a bit to read. Wide eyes reflect on the screen as I read the headline. It's a photo of Music & Life Magazine confirming that his divorce to Amelia Stanford has been settled. The only thing his caption says is that he and Amelia have both decided it was best to go their separate ways and ask for privacy during this time.

Well, damn. I lean back, my shoulders sagging. Knox didn't mention this when I asked him how his trip went.

I think back to all the recent gossip shared about him and remember seeing a photo of him with another woman, along with allegations of cheating. Is she the reason he asked for a divorce? I know nothing about his life, and here I am harboring a crush on him, which grows every time I see him.

He's different than I imagined, and he's definitely not the grouch that first showed up at the bar with Axel a few weeks ago. For some reason, I wanted to make him smile from the first moment I met him. I felt so bad for all the crap they were saying. He's proven to be a good guy, from defending me at Clarke's when the men were disrespectful to bringing dinner yesterday when he heard I was sick. Someone who wasn't kind-hearted wouldn't go through the trouble.

I shake my head, a sad smile on my lips. I can't help but believe I'm not the woman he wants to restart his life with. He's a friend, I think, or he just feels bad because I mentioned how hard it's been to make friends in this town and took it upon himself to mend that.

Either way, it doesn't matter. I like hanging out with him, and it's nice to have someone to talk to outside of the bar. I'm not letting a few rough bumps stop me from enjoying this life and attempting to make some friends. If there's one thing I've learned in life, it's that you fight for the dream until it becomes a reality. Then, you fight to keep that reality the best version for you.

When I finish my coffee, I take medicine I picked up at the pharmacy yesterday and shower. I can only stay home and rest for so long. Besides, I need to go to work tonight. Tips are the majority of my income, and with the holidays around the corner, I'm saving to send gifts to Geema and my parents, although I'm hoping they'll be able to stop here for Christmas. It's too hectic of a time for me to ask for a holiday, and I've been told Christmas is amazing here.

I tread slowly to my car, careful not to slip on a patch of ice, and let out a breath once I'm sitting safely in my car. They weren't kidding when they said the snow starts early here. It's only November, and the ground has already accumulated snow for a few days. It's beautiful, but driving in it scares the heck out of me.

I stop for another cup of coffee after running a few errands. The warmth as I enter Cup-O-Joe makes me want to stay in here all day and read.

"Hey," I hear a voice call out from somewhere next to me. I turn to find Axel sitting at a table.

"Hey." I smile at him and place my order before walking toward him. "How are you?"

"Good. Taking a break from the ranch, so I came to grab some coffee." Axel was the first friend I made here, building a relationship throughout the few months I've lived here. I know if I ever need anything, I can call him, and he'll make himself available to help me.

"Cool. I was running errands and stopped by for a latte. It's cold out there," I shiver.

Laughing, he nods. "It's only gonna get colder. You better bundle up because winter here is no joke."

"I see that. It's not even Thanksgiving, and the snow is falling. It is beautiful though," I stare out the window, admiring the white blanket on the ground. "Hey," I turn back to look at him. "How's Knox? I heard about the divorce."

"He's doing okay. If I know him, he'll spend a few days locked up at home." He shakes his head as if he didn't approve of his brother's coping mechanisms. "Why?" He raises his eyebrows.

"I was curious. He's been nice to me, and I wanted to make sure he was okay," I throw a bullshit excuse, and Axel doesn't buy it.

A wide smile appears on his face. "Really? And here I thought I was going to gain a sister-in-law I actually liked," he winks as he teases me.

"What? No!" I feel the heat of my blush all over my face and neck. Axel laughs, his head tilting back as his cackles echo around the coffee shop. It's not lost on me that he said a sister-in-law he actually likes. I take it Knox's family wasn't Amelia's biggest fans.

"I'm only teasing you, Ainsley, but I wouldn't lie and say I'd be upset if you two had something."

"Are you playing matchmaker?" I tilt my head.

"All I'm saying is that I know what's good for him," he winks and finishes off his coffee. "Well, I gotta go. I'll see you later if I can drag my brother out of the house for a drink." Axel stands from his seat, putting on his cowboy hat. It amazes me how everyone here wears their hats wherever they go, including Clarke's at night.

Sure, I'm from Texas, but Dallas isn't a rancher town, and I *am* now living in The Cowboy State.

"You're a good brother," I compliment him.

"I don't do anything he wouldn't do for me," he shrugs. "We've always had each other's backs, and that's not going to change anytime soon."

Hoping he could get Knox to go to Clarke's tonight, I head home to eat something and rest before having to work this afternoon.

I've spent the first two hours of work checking the door every time someone new walks in. I'm officially obsessing over seeing Knox tonight. Trying to focus on something else, I organize the glasses behind the bar and make sure my customers don't need any refills or want to put in a food order.

I surrender to the idea that he won't be coming tonight, probably wanting to keep to himself for obvious reasons. The rumor mill has been high today around this town with people blatantly talking about his divorce. Besides, it's not like I won't run into him again, that seems to be our thing.

"Hey." I turn around, smiling at Axel and see Knox taking a seat next to him.

"Hi, guys."

"How are you feeling?" Knox asks as Axel looks between us.

"Better, thanks. I'm probably close to getting high on cold medicine, but it's keeping me on my feet. I don't think I could stay home another night," I ramble, wiping the bar top. "Anyway, beer and whiskey?" I ask, looking between them.

Axel chuckles and nods. I roll my eyes at him and serve their drinks, keeping my hands in the pockets of my waist apron to stop myself from fidgeting with a pen.

I'm aware of Knox's gaze as I work, smirking in his direction when I catch his eyes. We don't speak as the weekend crowd picks up, but he's present, giving me attention that I'm not sure he wants to really give me.

I shake away those negative thoughts and do the job I love, chatting with customers, moving to the music, and laughing. I head toward Knox when he waves me over, noticing Axel's absence.

"Do you want another round?" I ask, leaning forward on the bar.

"Please." A subtle smile appears on his face, dissipating my nerves. "Thanks," he says as I finish pouring the whiskey. "You're really feeling better?" he adds with furrowed brows.

"Yes, honestly. I slept through the night and into the morning, which helped big time. How are you?" I give him a sideways glance.

"Good."

"I heard about the divorce," I whisper. "If you need someone to talk to, I'm a good listener." I leave it at that, wanting him to know he has a support system outside of his family, even if I am just one person and not so much a system.

"Thanks, but I'm okay."

"Good," I perk up, about to walk away when his hand rests on mine. I face him, my eyes meeting his, intense and sad.

"I appreciate it, more than you know." He squeezes my fingers before releasing me, but that doesn't remove the hold he has on me. Knox Bentley is different than I imagined, in a good way, and I'm having a hard time keeping my feelings platonic.

chapter 9

Knox

I stare out my patio doors, steaming cup of coffee in my hand, as I watch the snow fall in the early morning hours. Winter came early this year. This is foreign to me after living in Los Angeles for so many years. I run a hand through the mussed waves of hair, taking a moment to pause before the day starts.

The weekend has been full of divorce talk on social media, articles sharing the news on online media sites, and the fans in a frenzy because their *favorite* couple has split up.

If they only knew…

As for me, the weekend has been freeing. For the first time in years, I felt like I wasn't attached to something holding me back. As much as I wanted to stay in for a few days, I took Axel up on his offer to go to Clarke's on Saturday after he mentioned Ainsley asked about me. I can't stop thinking about her—the shine in her eyes, her laughter, the way she looked wrapped in her blanket, the shape of her breasts when the blanket fell around her waist as she ate.

Fuck.

I adjust myself on the outside of my sweatpants, half-tempted to jump in the shower and rub one like a teen boy.

I grab my phone from my pocket and open Instagram. Ignoring all the notifications but one, I click on her profile and send a private message. I've never been one to slide into DMs, but since I don't have her number, yet, I'm left with no choice.

Hoping she answers quickly, I jump in the shower in case she'll want to spend the morning with me. Today is a new start in all aspects of my life. Harris told me RWB Records is releasing a statement this morning about our professional separation, and I'm ready to release my own afterward.

I grab my phone from the bathroom vanity after wrapping a towel around my waist. Drops of water dribble down my face from my hair and land on my phone screen, but I unlock my phone and open my Instagram app.

Hard_Ains: why are you awake already?
KnoxBentleyOfficial: I'm a morning person.
So? Are you free today?
Hard_Ains: I guess... although my bed is warm and you're interrupting my sleep

I smirk. Tempted to write something inappropriate, I keep my focus on my plans for the day.

KnoxBentleyOfficial: let's go snow tubing. I promise it'll be fun. I'll even take you for coffee
Hard_Ains: did someone say coffee?! I'm up!

I chuckle and shake my head. I can just imagine her jumping from bed.

KonxBentleyOfficial: i'll pick you up. dress in warm layers

KnoxBentleyOfficial: and what's up with Hard in your name? Is this part of that G-Money phase in your life?

Hard_Ains: hahaha— funny guy. My last name is Harding. G-Money is only reserved for my Geema but if you're lucky you'll see my gangster side

KnoxBentleyOfficial: i'm gonna have to see this, lucky or not

Hard_Ains: we'll see ;) ok want to meet at the coffee shop for coffee before we go?

Hard_Ains: well duh if we meet at the coffee shop it's for coffee

KnoxBentleyOfficial: I'll pick you up

Hard_Ains: oh ok you already mentioned that yeah? I need coffee stat see ya in a bit then

I grin widely as I think about her. God, she rambles a lot, even in text. The image of her rapping makes me chuckle. I don't know if I deserve her or not, but she's worth a shot. If I'm going to reevaluate everything in my life and start fresh, that includes the possibility of another woman in my life, one that I choose to have by my side. We all deserve a chance at happiness.

I get dressed and grab my keys from the counter in the kitchen before heading out to pick up Ainsley. Every winter, we'd go snow tubing on our property after we finished chores. Snow has always been my favorite and something I missed when living between California and Nashville. Now, I actually have the time to live, and I want to take advantage of that. My career will fall into place with time.

Ainsley opens the door before I knock, bouncing on her toes. "Hey."

"Are you excited?" I tease, lifting my eyebrows.

"You promised coffee, and I never kid when it comes to my morning cup. Then, you can take me wherever you want," she smirks, her lips pinching together.

I lick my lips and stare at her for a second. Her jeans, tucked into her snow boots, hug her hips and legs while a thick, tan sweater covers her upper body.

"Come on. I've got big plans for us today." I grab her hand to pull her out the door, but she holds me back.

"Let me grab my coat," she raises her eyebrows, eyes twinkling with mischief as she looks down her body.

Well, I'll be damned, is she flirting with me?

"Hurry." I bounce on my toes, feeling like a kid who is skipping a school day. It's been a long time since I've been excited about something and it's thanks to the woman fighting with her coat. "Here," I reach out for her coat. "Let me help you."

I hold it open as she turns around and slips her arms into the sleeves. I run my hands down her arms, squeezing her hands.

"Let's go," my words come out deeper than intended.

Swiping her long ponytail away from the collar, she faces me with intensity in her eyes. "Knox."

"Time's a-tickin'," I interrupt her, not wanting to hear any excuses and pulling myself together.

I drive toward my parents' property and grab the inflated tubes in one of the covered barns before heading further into the mountains.

"I'm so excited," she squeals when I'm back in the truck as she warms her hands around the cup of coffee we grabbed on the way.

"I love tubing." I park the car, and she's out before I close the driver's door.

"I've never done it, but I've always seen pictures, and it looks like so much fun." Her southern accent becomes more apparent as she helps me carry one of the tubes.

"Okay, how about you show me what to do?" she asks.

"Let's climb a little higher," I lead the way up the hill.

"Thank goodness I'm not afraid of heights." She falls into step with me as we trek through the snow.

"Okay," I stop walking once we're in a part of the hill that's flat. "It's easy. You sit and kick forward a bit and just enjoy the ride."

"Enjoy the ride," she muses. "I like that." She tilts her head and pops her hip out a bit. "Okay, show me," she says again, her excitement laced in her words as she bounces on her toes.

I sit on the tube and push forward, rushing downhill. The wind blows past me, the cold hitting my ears as the exhilaration of letting go takes over.

I stand at the bottom of the hill and look up at Ainsley, ready to go. Smiling, I watch her fly through the snow as her screams fill the open space. Her tube comes to a stop a few feet past me, and she's quick to her feet.

"That was a blast!" She pulls the tube behind her until she's standing in front of me. "Ready to go again?"

"Hell yeah," I stare at her, soaking in her sunshine. She's the golden rays of hope fighting through the dull gray in my life.

She grips my hand and pulls me back up the hill, the warmth of her glove filling me as I see the possibility of a happy life.

Ainsley drops onto the tube and slides down, arms up in the air before they quickly shoot down to grab the handles on the sides. I guffaw watching her almost tip over.

When she's out of my way, I jump on, ready to meet her at the bottom of the hill. The rush of being out here, surrounded by nature and privacy, drips life back into me like an IV. Once I reach the bottom, I stand with the tube in my hand and feel something hit my back. Turning around, I find Ainsley laughing hysterically to herself.

"Are you sure you want to play this game?" I lift a brow and grin.

"I have no idea what you're talking about." She squares her shoulders and juts her chin.

Silently, I bend and pack a snowball into my hand, grateful for the thick gloves I grabbed on my way out of the house.

She trembles again, and I take a step back. "Are you cold?"

"A little. Sorry," she shrugs.

"Don't be, let's go. Do you work tonight?" I grab both tubes by the handles and hold her hand with my free one.

"Yeah."

"Let's pick up lunch and eat at my place. I can take you to work after," I offer.

"I can drive, and I need to change anyway."

"I'll take you home to change, but I want to drive you to work. I have no other plans tonight than to be in your company, even if you're tending the bar," I state. She shakes her head, but a smile covers her face.

"What do you want for lunch?" she changes subjects.

"How about we grab tacos from Dorado Grill?"

"I love that place," she exclaims.

"Perfect." I don't let go of her hand as we walk to my truck, wanting to hold on to this feeling.

Since I've met Ainsley, she's snuck her optimism into my life. When I felt like I was hitting rock bottom, she smiled my way and has held on so far. I don't know where my life is going, but I do know that I want to get to know the woman next to me.

"Do you know what you want from Dorado?" I ask her as I sit in my truck.

"Their steak tacos in soft shells."

"Awesome. I'll place an order, so it's ready when we get there." I hit call, and my Bluetooth speaker rings in the cab. I order our food and drive toward the center of town.

"Tubing was so much fun," Ainsley says. "Thanks for asking me to come with you."

"I'm glad you agreed. I loved coming here as a kid, even when I was a teen. Axel and I used to spend hours sliding down the hills, competing with each other over who rode the fastest."

"I can imagine you two arguing about that," Ainsley interrupts me with a chuckle.

"I always won," I deadpan.

"I'm sure he'd say the opposite." She tosses her head back on the headrest. I chance a glance her way, taking in the slope of her neck, her plump lips and blue eyes smiling as they stare out the windshield. She turns toward me and catches my eyes. I wink at her before looking back at the road ahead of us and getting to Dorado Grill as soon as possible, so I can spend more time with her in the privacy of my home.

chapter 10

Ainsley

My lips still feel the ghost of Knox's kiss. When he held me, I wanted to let myself fall into him, get lost in his woodsy scent and strong arms. I almost did, but then he broke the kiss, and I wanted to beg for more. It's been a long time since I've been kissed with equal parts tenderness and passion.

I can't help but sneak peeks at him while we eat. He catches me every time and simply smiles.

Stunning is an understatement when describing his home. Stone architecture on the outside with modern lines that give it the perfect balance between country and chic. The two-story home feels like a family home, and I wonder if he bought it with hopes that he and Amelia would live here.

I never thought I'd be attracted to a man who's been married before. It's a different experience, thought process. I find myself questioning things I never have.

"This fireplace is beautiful," I comment, looking at the flickering flames warming up the home. The kitchen opens up to the living room, making the perfect space for entertaining. The abundance of windows makes it feel more open and provides gorgeous views of the mountains and a lake.

"It's one of my favorite features in the house. I haven't had many opportunities to light it, so I take advantage." He leans back on the stool at the island, observing his home.

"It would be mine, too. Fireplaces are so cozy. I had one in my home in Colorado and wished my apartment here had one, but that would increase my rent." I shrug, wiping my mouth as I finish off my last taco.

"Yeah, Colorado gets really cold, too," Knox nods. "How long did you live there?"

"About six years. I was transferred for work to help start that branch," I explain, reminiscing. It was hard to leave Dallas, but I was excited about the new opportunity and living somewhere else.

"What did you do?" Knox shifts his body to face me.

"Marketing," I shrug.

"You don't like it?" He raises his eyebrows, his brown eyes more relaxed than a few weeks ago.

"I did, but I got burnt out. It was like starting a new company from scratch, and I love the creativity in marketing. Since I was a veteran from the Dallas office, I did a lot more paperwork and a lot less of the fun brainstorming and creating."

"I get that," he nods, pensive.

"I guess you could understand," I reply, wondering if artists lose their passion when it becomes a job.

"So," he claps his hands. "You gotta get to work, right?" He looks at the time on his phone.

"I do," I groan, tossing my head back. When Knox chuckles, I explain, "I love working at Clarke's, but it's been nice to relax."

"I'm glad." He grabs hold of my hand and kisses the inside of my wrist before clearing the plates. My body tingles, and I wish I could stay here with him for the rest of the afternoon.

"Let's get you home so you can change." He walks around the island until he's standing next to me. I take the hand he offers and stand, his body keeping me trapped between the counter and him. "Thank you for spending the morning with me." Knox's gaze bores into mine, searching for something only he's privy of.

"I really did have fun. I should be thankin' you…"

He shakes his head, stopping me from talking. "Trust me when I say that spending time with you has been the most fun I've had in years and the most 'me' I've felt in a very long time."

My heart is banging against my ribs, and my breathing is quick as his words sink in. I'm not sure why he feels that way with plain ole me, but it fills me with pride and also saddens me for the way he's been living. One look at Knox, and it's clear he isn't entirely happy with his life.

"I guess we're going to have to make sure your life is once again full of good times. No one should miss out on living the way they want." I tighten my hand around his and smile.

"I like you, Ainsley Harding." My breath catches in my throat when his free hand holds the side of my face, and his lips touch mine in a soft kiss. I close my eyes and lean into him, savoring the moment.

"Ready?" His question is husky. I nod, walking out of his house while keeping my hand in his.

I don't know Knox's backstory and what happened in his marriage, but I know I want to discover every part of him and be responsible for making him smile so freely again.

♪

Although I insisted I didn't need him to drive me to work, Knox was hellbent on bringing me, which means he'll be driving me home when my shift is over. I'll be lying if I say that doesn't add to my good mood as I work.

In between serving customers, Knox and I share secret glances and smiles. His fingertips graze mine as he grabs the glass from my hands after serving him another round. I shiver and look away, making sure no one is on to our game.

As much as I'm enjoying my time with Knox, neither of us need drama in our lives. Until I know where this is going, I don't want people in town starting rumors about our relationship.

"Hey, Ainsley, can you make me a margarita?" Jill, one of our waitresses, pops into the bar.

"Got it." I mix the ingredients, serving the margarita in a salt-rimmed glass and place it on the pick-up station on the side of the bar.

I assess the people sitting at the long counter, checking to see whose drink is low. As I sweep through the crowd, Knox's eyes catch my attention. He winks as he brings the rim of his glass to his lips. I'd give a lot to be kissing him right now. I feel heat cover my face as I think about his lips and roll my eyes when he laughs at my reaction, not oblivious to my blush.

Staying focused on work instead of the man sitting directly in the center of my bar, I make sure no one wants to place another order before organizing the back of the bar. Mondays are usually slower days, but with the cold weather, people in this town tend to seek shelter in a bar. Nothing like a good heater and alcohol to keep your body warm.

"Hey," I hear a male voice in front of me. I look up to see Eli sitting next to Knox, shaking his hand. "Hi, Ainsley." He nods in my direction.

"Hey, what can I get you?"

He looks at Knox's glass and back at me. "Gimme what he's having."

"Coming right up," I grab the bottle of scotch and fill his glass, setting it in front of him.

"Thanks," he winks, and I roll my eyes. Eli's always been a flirt. Knox sits up straighter, looking between the two of us with curious, narrowed eyes.

I shake my head, communicating without words. Eli has been a friend in the same way Axel has.

"Heard the good news. Cheers," I overhear Eli tell Knox.

"Thanks. I'm finally a free man." Knox's voice is even as he taps his glass with Eli's.

I watch the two friends drink and catch up, only hearing bits and pieces as I work. It seems like the label made the announcement like Knox mentioned would happen. Something about hearing that makes today more special. He chose me to spend such an important day with.

Smiling to myself, I work and sing along with the music sounding through the bar, replaying our kiss from earlier as the time passes.

♪

When Knox pulls into the parking lot in front of my apartment building, I unbuckle my seat belt and turn to him, tucking one leg under me. "Thanks for today."

"You don't need to thank me." He shakes his head.

I lean forward and kiss his cheek. "I want to thank you, accept it." I look up into his eyes in the dim cab illuminated by the street lights.

Knox groans and holds the back of my neck, bringing my lips to his, sweeping his tongue against mine as he drags me into a world where nothing else exists. My arms move around his neck as I scoot closer and I tug the ends of his hair. He moans into the kiss as I scrape my nails down his neck.

My entire body is ultra-aware and sensitive with the feel of him against me, his hand moving up and down my ribs.

"Damn, Ainsley." He pulls away slightly, catching his breath and leaning his forehead against mine. His hands cup my face, and he smirks. "I like kissing you." He gives me a peck. "I like spending time with you." Another kiss. "Did I mention I like *you*?" His lips swipe against mine again.

"You did, but you can say it again." I lean in and kiss him, wanting more.

Knox chuckles against my lips. "You don't let my fame affect you, and that means something to me."

His confession squeezes my heart. "You're a person," I shrug. "Your job shouldn't define you."

"But it does." He sighs and moves back, keeping his hands on my face. "I need you to understand that if we're going to continue spending time together. Eventually, people will notice."

I nod. "I know."

"I don't want to hide you. I made that mistake once, and I haven't forgiven myself yet. I don't want to hurt you."

I reach up and place my hand on his cheek, his beard tickling my palm. "It's okay. I understand that your life isn't as simple as others. When I first met you, I thought you were an ass, with your broody attitude and closed-off demeanor, but then you cracked a smile, and I knew there was more to you. It must not be easy to live the life you do, and I had heard some rumors, but you show up each day and live your life instead of letting other's opinions control you."

"You have no idea how much I've been controlled." His shoulders drop on a sigh, and his eyes close.

"Good thing you've taken back that power and started making decisions you want," I smile.

"You're always so positive," he states.

"I learned when I was a kid that we choose how we want to feel. My parents taught me that early on. They would tell me, it's okay to cry and feel sad. It's not okay to hold those emotions hostage for them to change me. I always carried that advice with me," I shrug, grateful my parents instilled that in my belief system from the beginning.

"I like that. I may have to borrow it."

"It's all yours." I reach for one of his hands on my face and bring it to my lap, clutching his fingers.

"When do you have a day off from work?" He holds my hand and drops the other to my thigh.

"Wednesday."

"Have dinner with me?" My stomach flips, and I nod with a smile. "Awesome." His wide grin tugs at my heart. "First, I need your number. As much as I like teasing you about your Instagram handle, I want to be able to call you."

"Hey now, my handle is just fine the way it is."

"You'll still have to show me your gangster side. I have a feeling you're bluffing," he teases.

I touch his chest with my finger and say, "You have to earn that right, but you just wait and see. I can rap like a pro."

Laughing, Knox looks at me, eyes twinkling. "I'm going to make sure you keep that promise." He grabs his phone. "Okay, tell me your number."

As soon as he saves it, my phone vibrates. "You've got mine now. If I can't make it to Clarke's tomorrow, I'll call you to tell you our plans for Wednesday."

"Sounds good." I hop out of his car, and he meets me by the hood before walking me up the stairs to my apartment.

"Goodnight," he whispers on a kiss.

"You, too."

When the door closes behind me, I jump with my arms flailing all around. Total nerd moment, but I have a date with Knox Bentley in two days. *Holy crap.*

chapter 11

Knox

"This view is gorgeous," Ainsley says as she stares out the gondola we're riding on, heading up to Oaks Resort. She looks stunning in black, tight jeans, heeled booties, and a cream over-sized sweater. Her blue eyes sparkle under the morning rays.

"It is," I look out the window at the snow-covered mountains and panoramic view of northern Wyoming.

I reserved one for us alone, grateful to not have other strangers with us, staring at me. When I asked her out, I wanted to do something special, different. As soon as I found out she was off the entire day, I planned an earlier date.

It was a greedy choice to plan something earlier so I could spend more time with her, but she makes me feel again after a long season of numbness. Ainsley is the type of woman you want around you. I knew a woman like that once, and I lost her. I've learned from my mistakes, and if life's given me the chance to be happy again, I'm grabbing it tightly.

She pulls out her phone and snaps a photo. "I want to make sure I keep a memory of this." She turns to look at me with a smirk and points her phone toward me and takes a picture. She giggles as she looks at it. "Not your best look, but I'm saving it."

"Let me see."

She shakes her head, so I lean forward across the gondola where she's sitting to snatch her phone, but she's quick. I leap for it, making the gondola shake a little.

"Oh, my God! Stop moving so much." Her wide eyes stare at me as she grips the sides, giving me a perfect chance to steal her phone away.

"Hey!" She's too slow, and I take a selfie.

"There, now you have a better picture." I hand back her phone and use her wrist to pull her toward me. She lands on my lap with a thud, and I wrap my arms around her waist. "This is better," I whisper in her ear.

Ainsley's chest rises and falls on a sigh, but she remains silent as she stares out the windows.

"Penny for your thoughts." I look up at her, her hand brushing through her hair before looking back at me.

"I'm confused." Her eyes cast down where my hands rest on the tops of her thighs. She places her hands over mine and smiles, but my body is tense as I wait for her to continue. "I like you, but you just got divorced, and you're in Everton while you figure out your next step. And then there's…" her voice trails off.

"There's what?" I push, holding her chin and turning her head to face me again.

"Your personal life and past aren't my business, but there's a reason the tabloids connected your divorce to another woman," she doesn't hold back, giving me what I asked for.

I flinch and shut my eyes. I let air slip from my mouth before opening my eyes and looking at her. "We don't know much about each other yet, and that's the point of spending time together. What I do know is that you bring some kind of spark into my life when it's been dull for a long time. Yes, part of the reason for my divorce was due to Reese, but it's not what you think."

"I just don't want history to repeat itself."

I know she's talking about her own relationship experiences, but when I say, "Me either," I'm talking about my own mistakes.

"I want to get to know you, learn what makes you smile, and hear you ramble on about your life and your favorite things. The last few years of my life have been chaos, which is why I've left the music industry. I'm not sure if I'll make a comeback or not, but for some time people will be watching my moves, guessing what decision I'll make.

"I don't want to hide you, but I also know what it's like to be talked about with assumptions and rumors and have your photo plastered everywhere. I wouldn't bring you into that life if I didn't have the intention of spending real time with you, but as soon as we step off this gondola and walk into the resort, we're making a statement. If you're not ready, we'll head back down, no hard feelings." I squeeze my arms around her, staring into her eyes.

"You said the resort serves breakfast all day long?" I nod. Her smile is a bright light, competing with the white snow shining below us. "I *love* breakfast food." She kisses me softly, her hair fanning around us.

"Day by day, I promise to tell you about my life because it is your business, but I just want to be in the present today." I run my hands up and down her back.

"I can live with that." She shifts on my lap, causing me to groan and her to giggle. "Oops." She winks, not one bit sorry.

I reach up and kiss her, biting her bottom lip. "You're gonna be really sorry if you don't stop."

She shivers in my arms, and I give her a crooked smirk, pleased with her reaction.

The gondola locks into the trail that stops at the resort, and I drop a kiss on the base of her throat before she stands. Adjusting myself, I walk out behind her and hold her hand. Ainsley doesn't back down or cower away from the eyes staring at us and whispering amongst each other. Instead, she looks up at me and beams. I wink, pulling her to me by the hand and wrapping my arm around her shoulder.

This woman has nothing to worry about if she thinks I prefer to spend my time with someone else.

♪

"Which has been your favorite place to perform?" Ainsley leans back in her seat, pushing her empty plate forward a bit so she can fold her hands on the table.

"Good one, I think the Opry. It's such a historic place and an honor to be invited to perform there. So many admirable musicians have performed on that stage, you can feel their energy when you walk into the auditorium," I respond.

"That must be amazing." She leans forward, propping her elbow on the table and resting her chin on her hand.

"My turn," I cross my arms and lean forward, the lingering smell of maple syrup from our waffles surrounding us. "Your favorite song."

Ainsley giggles and shakes her head. "I can't tell you."

"Fair is fair, I answer, and so do you." I shake my head. We've been at this game for thirty minutes, getting to know each other based on the questions we ask one another. So far, I know she fell and tore the skin on her knee when she was five because she jumped off a merry-go-round while it was still moving. She knows I have perfected my turkey call.

"Fine, but you can't laugh. I only say that because it goes with my whole gangster vibe." She rocks her shoulders up and down.

I bite down my laughter and widen my eyes, prompting her to speak.

"'The Real Slim Shady' by Eminem." She bites down on her lip.

"Really?" I tilt my head. "I wasn't expecting that, but I'm going to need you to sing this for me," I tease her.

"No, no," she shakes her head. "I only save my Marshall Mathers rapping for my empty apartment."

"We'll see," I smirk.

"Okay, what's your favorite number?" she changes subjects.

"Eight. I'm not sure why, but it always makes me feel lucky when I see it."

"Yeah, I don't know why people have favorite numbers, but it's interesting to learn what they are."

"Can I get you anything else?" the waitress interrupts.

"No, thank you. We're done," I reply and give her space on the table so she can gather our plates.

"Great. I'll bring the check then," she smiles at us, and I'm grateful she was professional while serving us.

"I guess that's our cue," Ainsley says.

"We can go back to my place and have a drink," I suggest, hoping to God she wants to spend more time with me.

"Sounds good."

I pay as soon as the waitress brings me the check and climb back on our private gondola as we return to the bottom of the mountain, Ainsley's hand in mine the entire time.

Once I'm driving back to my house, I press something on my phone and wait for her reaction.

"You didn't!" She slaps her thigh.

"Come on, I'll join you." Eminem's voice sounds through my sound system, and I notice her dancing out of the corner of my eye.

I chuckle when she starts singing, not missing a beat or lyric. Impressive. I sing the chorus with her, allowing her confident mood to sweep us away and back to my place.

"Oh man, I love that song." Her head hits the headrest with a thud.

"I used to listen to more of his music when I was younger, but then I discovered country music and fell in love with the genre," she shares.

"I've always loved it. It was all I wanted to do when I was a kid, and I fought for that dream." My lips turn up sadly, thinking back to the boy who wanted to be like Johnny Cash and Waylon Jennings.

"You should be proud of that." Ainsley reaches for my hand and holds on tight. "Not many people can say they've accomplished what you have."

"It's not always what it seems, though," I confess.

"I'm sure it's not. Being famous comes with many challenges, but you're sharing your passion with the world," she tries to comfort me.

I nod. "Maybe for some. I haven't written a song in a long time, let alone performed my own words in years."

"Really?" I feel her turn toward me. "How come?"

"Like I said, it's not always what it seems. When you sign your name to a label, you don't get to call the shots."

"Damn, I would hate to accomplish such an important dream and then not able to fully express myself."

"It's hard." I try to push away the sobering thoughts and focus on the woman next to me.

"Don't get me wrong, I enjoy your songs, but I can imagine how much better they'd be if you were singing words you felt passionate about," she comments. If I didn't think she'd understand me before, she proved me wrong. Ainsley surprises me more and more with each wisdom she shares.

"Anyway, I was thinking we can turn on the fire pit in my back porch. Are you too chicken to sit out in the cold?" I give her a sideways glance, challenging her.

"As long as I can wear my coat, I'm up for it."

"Perfect." I take us home as quickly as possible, ready to have her back in my arms.

chapter 12

Knox

As soon as we're inside my house, I ask Ainsley what she wants to drink. I'm surprised when she says scotch, and serve us each a glass. Then, I head out and uncover the fire pit, filling it with firewood and lighting it.

"Come on," I call Ainsley over as she looks at me from the open patio doors. She joins me, handing me my glass, and taking a seat close to the fire. I pull a chair close to hers and hit my cup to hers.

"Cheers," I say before taking a sip, allowing the amber liquid to warm me.

"This is beautiful." Her eyes sweep over the flames to the view of the mountains with the sun cast low, sinking behind them.

"I love it. It's my refuge." I know that when everything is wrong in the world, I can come here and put things into perspective.

"It's so peaceful," she adds, holding the glass between her thighs and reaching forward to warm her hands up by the fire.

"Come 'ere," I place the cup on the table to my left and reach my hand out to her. After setting her glass next to mine, I grab her hand and pull her to me until she's sitting on my lap.

I move my arms up and down her body, warming her up, as she stares out. When she leans back into me, I wrap my arms around her waist and kiss her neck. Ainsley moans softly, but my dick hears it. When she moves her hair to the side, I take that as an invitation to kiss her again. Her breathing becomes heavier as I nip her skin and continue to run my hands up and down her body.

She turns her head, catching my lips, the taste of whiskey on her breath as I stroke my tongue against hers. I press my hands into her hips and groan when I feel her shift on my lap. Next thing I know, she's completely turned around and straddling me, her hands in my hair and her lips moving down my jaw until her teeth graze my earlobe.

"Fuck," I growl, desperate to feel something more than the coat she's wearing.

"I know," she whispers before her lips land on mine again, and she kisses me with need. Her body pressed into mine makes it hard to control myself, and I want less barriers between us, but she calls the shots on how far we go.

Her breathing is erratic when she breaks away and places her head on my shoulder. "Sorry."

I chuckle. "I have no idea what you're apologizing for."

She looks up at me, making her body rub against my erection. "I got a little carried away." Her cheeks turn pink, and I rub a thumb across her soft skin. She's stunning with the sun's glow behind her, creating a halo over her blonde waves.

"You could do that again anytime you want." I drop a kiss on her swollen lips. "Anytime," I emphasize.

She shivers and grabs one of the glasses, no longer aware of which is hers or mine, and takes a drink of whiskey before tipping the cup and placing it on my lips so I can have some. Her eyes burn into mine, the playful Ainsley gone, a woman full of desire in her place.

"I'm not ready to go all the way, but I'd be lying if I said I didn't want to," she admits.

"We go at your pace." I don't want her to feel like I expect her to get naked and fuck me because of who I am.

"Thank you for that." With a final kiss, she stands and finishes off the scotch in the glass she's holding. "Let's go inside." She grabs my hand and leads me back inside, walking backward, so her sexy smile is still in my view.

Ainsley takes a seat on the floor in front of the fireplace and nods toward the guitar I have next to it. "Sing me a song no one else has heard," she requests.

I grab my guitar and tap on the wood, considering which song to play. "That not even my manager has heard?" I ask.

"Yup. One only you know about." She leans back on her hands with her legs crossed, patient while I choose a song.

Strumming the chords on the guitar, the house becomes quiet as I play a song I wrote years ago when I was in high school.

I've never felt as free
As when I'm with you
Underneath that oak tree
We claimed as ours,
Where we carved our love,
Made it immortal
Under the eyes of God and nature

Loving you is easy,
Your name on my lips,
Don't you see, you're perfect for me

I see you now with the same eyes
Though you're no longer mine,
The past is my present
While I keep your love alive,
You may no longer be mine,
But it's easy to forget
When I visit our oak tree
Where we carved our love

Loving you is easy,
Your name on my lips,
Don't you see, you're perfect for me,
Loving you is all I'll ever do
Until I'm buried beneath our oak tree

I finish off the final verse, eyes looking down at my hands as they play the last bit of the song. I hadn't played in months, swearing it would be a long time before I picked up my guitar again.

One request from Ainsley and I can't deny her this. It felt good, too. Playing something I wrote a long time ago, albeit not my best creation, was fun.

"That was really good," Ainsley smiles with pride, "and kinda sad. How come you've never shared that song?" She stretches her legs in front of her, massaging her knees.

"I wrote it when I was in high school. It's not up to par with professional standards," I explain.

"I doubt that. It's a really good song, and I'd jam to it if it came on my radio." I chuckle. "It's true," she exclaims. "Maybe not jam because again, unrequited love and all, but I'd sing along."

"Thanks." I take in her body, sweeping my gaze up her legs, pausing at her breasts before landing on her face. She watches me as I observe her, giving me this opportunity. "You're beautiful," I tell her.

"Thank you," she whispers.

I place the guitar on the floor next to me and grab her ankles, pulling her to me. Her screech fills my living room, and makes me laugh. Ainsley's hands hold my shoulders to steady herself as she tumbles over to me. I grab hold of her face and kiss her. I hold nothing back as I run my tongue over the seam of her lips, begging her to open for me. Tongues dancing, lips meshed together, and hands roaming, I cup her ass and lift her body enough to position her over me.

My hands tangle in her loose hair and tugging to angle her head so I can deepen the kiss. I swallow up her moans, wanting to hear more of her sounds. I move my hands down slowly, feeling the sides of her breasts and brushing my thumbs over her nipples through her sweater. Her body pushes into me when I do, encouraging me.

I move my lips from hers and kiss down her jaw and neck, finding that spot behind her ear and testing how crazy it makes her. Ainsley squirms when I suck, and my dick grows in my jeans.

I cup her breasts, keeping her top as a barrier, and she arches into my hands as her lips seek mine. Her kiss is desperate and controlled at the same time, knowing exactly what she's doing. Her nails scratch the back of my neck, and she bites my lower lip, causing me to growl. That's fucking hot.

Ainsley gives me one more kiss and moves her head back enough to stare at my eyes. Her chest rises and falls in quick sprints, my hands still cupping her breasts. I give her a playful squeeze and move them down until they land on her hips. Her eyes travel down our bodies to where her body sits on mine and our legs tangle. When her eyes sweep back to mine, she gives me the sexiest smirk I've ever seen and groan.

"You're killing me," I say, then shake my head. "Actually, scratch that, you're giving me life again."

Her chest swells as she sucks in a breath and slowly lets it go. She cups my face and rubs her thumb across my cheek. Part of me wants to look away from her probing eyes, but I know with her I can show who I really am without judgment.

Her gentle caress continues as her fingers lightly brush my lips, and I shiver. She moves to my eyebrows, tracing their shape before circling my face and coming back to my lips.

"I could kiss you for hours." She pecks my lips. "I want to do a lot more than kissing," she confesses with another kiss. "But what I like most is talking to you, being in your presence." I close my eyes to still my racing heart and feel her lips touch my forehead.

Only one other woman has ever treated me like this, and the guilt for thinking about her in this moment swallows me. I shake my head and expel a breath. If I want to move forward with Ainsley, I need to be honest with her.

"I think I should tell you why I got divorced."

Ainsley looks down at me, her expression serious as she nods and moves off me, sitting across from me. I run a hand through my hair as I collect my thoughts.

"Before I say anything, I need to ask that what I tell you stays between us, please. This can't come out." I shake my head with a pained expression.

"I promise." She gives me a small smile and grabs hold of my hand.

"Thanks." This will probably change her idea of me, and I rather get this over with now before what I feel for her becomes more serious.

"Before I became a well-known artist, I was dating a woman. We were together for two years, and she supported me in every step of my rise to stardom, if we must call it that. We never made our relationship public, especially when I gained popularity, so we wouldn't get thrown into the drama of it all. I wanted to protect her." I blow out air and comb back my hair.

"Anyway, when RWB Records heard my demo and called me, I was excited as hell. Harris, my manager, worked with them, read over the contract, negotiated on my behalf. He got me the best deal for an emerging artist with no real following. I had no right to be picky, and the offer looked amazing when I had no other deal thrown my way after years of trying and RWB Records being one of the most coveted labels.

"Anyway, after talking it through with Harris, we both decided it was in my best interest to sign with them. It didn't take long for people to learn who I was and my fanbase to grow. Reese and I kept our relationship hidden, but we had no doubt we wanted to be together. I loved her with everything I had." It's hard to share this with another woman, but Ainsley needs to know. She listens on, giving nothing away as I speak.

"One day, my publicist called me in for a meeting, telling me about a pop star and how she was a breakout artist at the time. I didn't understand why she was telling me that until she finished talking and it all clicked. RWB

Records is connected to Amelia's label, sister companies let's call it. They were working on merging pop and country music, wanting to become a powerhouse. Our publicists set Amelia and me up. I had no choice but to marry her. The label owned everything about my image when I signed my rights to them a few months prior.

"All I wanted was to be with Reese, and at that moment, I realized how dirty this career was and that I was nothing more than a puppet to them. A money maker. When I told Reese the situation, she broke up with me. She wouldn't be the other woman, and I couldn't get her to understand she wouldn't be. In her eyes, I was going to be a married man, and those vows meant as much to her if they were real or for show." I rub my fingers over my forehead.

"I sold my soul to the devil without realizing it, and I was stuck performing songs I hated, playing up an image that wasn't me, and married to a woman I never loved. The worst part is that I broke the heart of the one woman I loved and my own heart in the process. I lost myself, lost the passion and respect I had for the industry, and slowly began hating everything about myself and my life. Four years was too long to play this game I'd never win, and I decided to take my life back into my own hands. This is where I am now." I shrug, searching Ainsley's eyes for some kind of clue as to what she's thinking.

"So that's why you saw Reese recently," she states instead of questions, knowing damn well what the answer is.

I nod. "I went to tell her I was getting a divorce as if that would change what I did, make me a hero, but I needed to tell her."

"You still love her," she states with a sad smile.

"She was the first woman I ever loved and truly wanted to build a life with. Our end was unconventional, so I felt like I never got closure. I won't lie and say I don't care for her anymore, but when I saw her last, I received the closure we both needed. She's with someone now. She's happy, which was all I ever wanted for her. Yes, she's the reason I wanted to take my life back because I knew what it felt like to have it all and wanted that again." I reach for Ainsley's hands.

"I think a part of me will always feel guilty for what I did. I never thought of myself as a heartbreaker, and I became that years ago. It made me hate myself." I've never told anyone exactly how I felt and continue to feel. I never expressed the extent of my disappointment and sadness.

"Maybe we should take a step back, so you could have time to figure out exactly what you want," her suggestion is a punch to my core.

I shake my head. "If I wasn't ready, I wouldn't have asked you out."

"I understand and believe that, but I don't want to get in the way of anything."

"You're not. That's just it. I left Nashville, left the music scene, angry and resentful because it took everything I cared about away from me. It took away the one thing I've always wanted, which was a happy life. It turned success into something dirty. I got here, feeling sorry for myself, giving Axel a hard time to get me out of this house. Then, I met you, and something about you made me smile again. You reminded me of everything I lost, and at first, I was angrier at myself, but then it's as if I started to remember what it felt like to be happy." I want her to understand that seeing her, whether at Clarke's, the grocery store, or a planned date, makes me see things differently.

"I won't come second." She shakes her head. "After what my ex-boyfriend did, I want to make sure the next man I end up with is fully present for me."

"I won't make that mistake again. Let me show you." I lace our fingers together.

"I really like you, Knox, and I knew that your life was complicated. Because of that, I think it's important that you find happiness again, but not because of me. I can't be responsible for making you happy, but if you need someone, I'm here. Promise." She leans forward, and her lips ghost over mine.

I hug her to me and murmur against her hair. "I like you too, Hard_Ains, and I'm going to prove to you that I mean it when I say you're the woman I want in my life." Her arms wrap around my middle and squeeze tightly.

I may always hold Reese somewhere in my heart, but I know we'll never have a future. I want her to be happy, even if it's without me. I'm still working through those emotions, mostly on the anger of my reality, but Ainsley has dawned new light on my life, brightening it so I could see in the dark. I'm going to fight for her, something I never did for Reese.

"I guess I should take you home." I lean back and look into her blue eyes.

"Yeah," she nods, biting her lip.

"I meant what I said. I still feel guilty for my past, but I've learned from it. I know when I've found a woman worth fighting for, and I'm gonna fight for your trust," I assure her.

Ainsley's eyes crinkle as she smiles. "I hope so," she whispers.

When I drop Ainsley off at home, I make a promise to myself to figure out what I want to do with my life, work through my stuff, so I can have a life I'm proud of. Reese is my past, my lessons, and I finally believe I can have a future.

chapter 13

Ainsley

I dry the glass in my hand with a towel as I stare at the wood grain pattern on the countertop. For the last two days, I've been distracted thinking about Knox. I was so close, and then reality dumped a bucket of ice water over my head. I knew his life was complicated, but I wasn't expecting all of that.

"Hey."

I jump when I hear the greeting and look up, hand still inside the glass. I find the eyes of the person I was thinking about, smiling.

"I didn't mean to scare you," Knox says as he settles on a stool in front of me, chuckling lightly.

"I spaced out. How are you?" I set the glass down and drop the towel on the shelf beneath the bar top.

"Good, thought I'd come see my favorite bartender," he winks.

I smile, shaking my head. When he told me everything he went through, my heart broke for him. I can't imagine being in a position where I have no control over my destiny. It broke further when I realized he still wasn't over his first love, and a girl can't compete with that.

"Well, here I am," I open my arms. "Whiskey?" I tilt my head.

"Actually, I'll take a beer today." I nod and grab a bottle of Sam Adams, popping the cap and placing it in front of him along with a glass.

I thought he'd come by yesterday, but I told him he needed to take his time to figure out what he feels and where he wants his life to go, so I don't know why I expected him to run to Clarke's the day after our date with the way it ended. I can't be responsible for anyone's happiness, no one can, so when I told him he had to find that joy himself, I meant it. It hurt to make that choice, but ultimately, it's for the best.

The truth is, I like him a lot and knowing he has feelings for someone else hurts, even if he says I'm the person he wants in his life.

"How are you?" he asks with a serious tone.

"I'm good." I nod. It's not a lie, I tell myself. I'd say I'm more confused, knowing he likes me but feeling as if he hasn't fully gotten closure with his past and unsure of how you get that type of closure. Will he always wonder, what if?

"Can I get a beer?" I look to the left where a man is waving me down. I nod, making my way to him so I can take his order. More and more people trickle in, hiding from the cold, and my slow shift suddenly becomes hectic. Thankful for the crowd, I get to work, enjoying a job I never thought I'd be good at but was always curious about. Some people bartend while in college. I never did like doing what others did, so bartending can be my post-career job.

Throughout the night, I sneak glances at Knox, who says hi to some of the locals that approach him. He looks relaxed, so handsome too, especially when he combs back his wavy hair and smiles genuinely. That kind of smile brightens up his face, adding a twinkle in his dark eyes.

"You're staring," someone whispers in my ear and I startle. What is it with people sneaking up on me today?

I look up to find Axel laughing. "Asshole," I mutter. "And no, I wasn't," I play it off with a shrug, looking in another direction.

"Yeah, right," he continues to chuckle.

"Whatever." I roll my eyes.

"He likes you," Axel confides, but I shake my head.

"He's still in love with Reese."

With furrowed brows, Axel looks at me and then at his brother a few seats down. "He told you that?"

"Not exactly, but he told me what happened between them and with Amelia," I whisper. "It's obvious he isn't over her," I confide in him.

"Give him time. These last few years have been hard on him, with not being able to really say what happened and living a life that wasn't real, but he's moving on." I'm grateful for Axel's attempt to make things seem better, but a few words of encouragement won't magically heal the heart.

"Thanks. You want a beer?"

"Yeah, I'm gonna go sit over there." He taps the counter before making his way to Knox.

I take a moment to look at them and observe their relationship. I'm an only child, but I'm sure having a sibling you can count on is amazing. Fortunately, I have a family I can count on, even if we're states apart.

"What are you doing for Thanksgiving?" Axel asks when I serve his beer.

"I don't know, rest," I shrug. "And spend the day eating homemade pumpkin pie." I rub my belly, causing the Bentley brothers to laugh.

"No way," Axel says, looking at his brother as they communicate with their eyes. "Thanksgiving should be spent with family, and I know yours is away, so you're coming over to celebrate with us," he finishes off.

"What? No, no." I shake my head, waving a hand in front of them.

"Yes," Knox speaks up with authority.

"I appreciate it, but it's just another day, and I'm looking forward to relaxing at home." I play it off. I won't interrupt their family dinner by inviting the new girl in town.

"Ainsley, don't be stubborn. We'll be more than happy to have you," Knox smiles.

I cross my arms and narrow my eyes. "I'm not being stubborn."

Knox leans forward and whispers, "You are, and you look cute as hell when you are."

I widen my eyes and lock my jaw while Axel laughs. He slaps a hand on Knox's shoulder, shaking his head while others look his way to see what's causing a ruckus.

I look away, not wanting people to put two and two together, and head to the person flagging me down with a ten-dollar bill in their hand.

It doesn't take long for Knox to call me over again, ordering another beer and making sure I understand how serious he is. "Thanksgiving isn't meant to be spent alone. We have more than enough space for you and would be honored if you came. Bring your homemade pumpkin pie, if it makes you feel better. Hell, bring two if you want to eat one all by yourself, but you're coming to spend it with us."

"He won't take no for an answer," Axel pipes up.

"Fine, thank you," I nod, heart pounding.

"Good," Knox leans back with a satisfied smile.

Throughout the rest of the night, I watch as he and Axel talk, laugh, and hang out with friends. I take pride in seeing Knox happy, hoping I have something to do with that. It's as if slowly, he's coming back to the person he was and observing that from the outside is fascinating.

♪

I look around Main Street as I stroll down the sidewalk. All the buildings are made of wood siding, some in its natural color, others painted in beige. It gives the town a very Old West feel as if any moment now a cowboy were to walk out of swinging doors of a bar and climb on his horse.

I giggle to myself. I'm such a nerd. Clearly, we're in the twenty-first century, but a vintage charm resides here and is instilled in the locals. I've been told it's the cowboy way from ancestors that lingers in the area. As spooky as that can sound, I believe it.

Taking advantage of the clear morning, I walk around and enjoy some sunshine despite the snow on the mountains lining Everton. When I have a day off or the morning free, I love exploring the town. There's still so much to learn about it and its history.

I step into my next destination—an antique store. An employee greets me, and a few people linger as I take a look around at what they have. I see old lamps with stained glass shades, copper vases, and wooden chests. I squeeze through the make-shift aisles, careful not to knock anything with my purse or butt.

I find more antiques, like old gardening tools, furniture, and creepy dolls. I never was a fan of those. This place is full of articles from different eras, all showing a vast history of the people from this town, and some, I'm sure, from further away.

I search a table that has random things placed on it, and I smile when I see a cardboard case with Johnny Cash's face on it. I lift the case and tip it to the side, a vinyl disc sliding out. I hold in my excitement, not wanting to scream and interrupt the people shopping peacefully.

Turning it over, I search for a price but don't see one. Hoping it's within budget, I take another look around in case there's something else worth grabbing. My eyes light up when I see something that is perfect, and I walk up to the register to ask for the price of the record and pay for my things, knowing I got a steal.

As I walk out of the shop, my phone rings. I fish it out of my purse, struggling with the gifts I'm carrying and ignoring the curious looks from people walking past me. I huff and look at my phone, furrowing my eyebrows.

"Geema?" I see my grandmother's face practically pressed against the screen of my phone when I answer and laugh. "Are you video calling me?"

"Yes, your cousin taught me."

"How is Andrew?" I ask.

"Oh, good. He has his first girlfriend. You know, middle school love," she shares family news.

"Okay, Geema, can you move the phone a little away from your face so I can see more than your eyes and nose?" I reach my car and pop the trunk, placing my belongings in there before settling in the driver side to talk to my grandmother, turning on the heat to full blast.

"How's that? You look beautiful, sweetheart," my grandma's eyes brighten.

"Thanks, and that's much better. Now I can see your entire face. How are you?" I sigh as the comfort of talking to her sweeps over me.

"I'm good. How about you? How's life in the wild, wild west?"

I laugh. It's as if she read my earlier thoughts. "It's great. I needed this, and I'm feeling more and more at home. I just found the perfect Christmas gift for you," I shimmy in my seat.

"I'm so happy to hear that. We miss you here, but I know you're happy and that's all that matters. Well, that and this gift you're telling me about. Show me," she demands.

"Nope." I shake my head. "You're going to have to wait 'til it arrives. No cheatin'." I nod once and scream, grabbing my chest with my free hand. "What in God's name?" I look out the door window and find Knox standing on the outside of my car, head tilted back in a fit of laughter.

"Are you okay?" Worry laces my grandmother's voice.

"Yes, but someone else might be about to die," I say as I roll down the window so he can hear me.

Knox continues to laugh as he tries to speak, clutching his stomach. "What are you doing, taking a selfie?"

"I'm talking to my Geema." I turn the phone a bit to show him.

"Who's that, sweetie? He's handsome." My eyes widen in mortification as her voice rings around us.

Knox chuckles. "Geema! He can hear you."

"Oh, well, I was never shy around the boys. Let me take a good look at him." She squints her eyes and adjusts her glasses. I'm about to die.

Mortified, I turn the phone, heat prickling my neck. Arguing with her is pointless. "It's the infamous Geema.

It's very nice to meet you, ma'am," Knox bows his head a bit, causing me to laugh. She's not the Queen.

"So, I'm infamous, huh? How much time have you been spending with my granddaughter?" Her words are curious, and I'm afraid of what she'll say next.

"As much as she gives me." Knox doesn't flinch.

"Good girl, make him work for it." I could imagine her patting my hand in solidarity.

"Oooh-kay, Geema, I'll call you later. Preferably when I'm home alone, and you can't embarrass me anymore."

"Have fun," she sing-songs. I end the call and look at Knox with a sheepish grin.

"She's a riot," Knox says.

"Ugh." I drop my head to the steering wheel.

"I never thought I'd see Ainsley Harding embarrassed."

I roll up my window, ignoring his comment, and open the door to stand outside. "I guess there's a first time for everything," I deadpan, which only makes him laugh more.

"What are you up to?" Knox's hands sneak into his pockets.

"I was Christmas shopping."

"Already?" His eyebrows pop up.

"I need to send the gifts to Texas, so I'm getting an early start. I found the perfect gift for Geema." I clap my hands and walk to my trunk. I pull out the vinyl album and show Knox.

"Is she a Johnny Cash fan?" He nods, impressed.

"Biggest fan and she refuses to listen to music on anythin' that isn't vinyl," I explain. "It's perfect. I can't wait for her to receive it. I just wish I could see her face when she does. Maybe we can video chat now that she's learned how to." I think of ways to be as present as possible when she opens her gift.

"You miss her, right?" Knox shifts, crossing one leg over the other.

"Yeah, but I'm used to it by now. I've lived away from home for so long."

"It's still hard," he nods in understanding.

"Yeah," I trail off. "So, what are you up to?"

"Enjoying the sunshine." He faces the sky, the light hitting the few grays in his beard and temples.

"It is nice out—cold, but nice," I wrap my arms around my body.

"What else did you buy?" He juts his chin toward my opened trunk.

"Only the coolest thing ever," I brag and reach for the antique sled.

"Is that a sled?"

"Duh. I would expect more from you seeing as you're from around here," I tease. "I thought it would be so cool to try."

"Um, would it work?" He furrows his brows and reaches out to hold the old, wooden sled.

"It looks like it's in good condition. Only one way to find out," I challenge.

"I'm pretty sure this is for kids. It'll probably hold you, but it definitely won't hold my weight."

I cross my arms and give him an offended look. "Probably hold me?"

"Um, what I mean is, it's for kids. I'm sure it will hold you. Shit." He runs a hand through his hair, and I cackle.

"I'm only kidding."

"That was wrong." He blows out a breath, shaking his head.

"What do you say? Are you up for testing this old thing?" I point to the sled in his hands.

"Hell, yeah."

"Great, hop in and tell me which way to go." I grab the sled and put it back in the trunk before sliding into the driver's seat. I notice Knox shaking his head through the rearview mirror as he walks around my car and sits in the passenger side.

Following his directions, we go back to where we went tubing. I shiver as I step out of the car, not dressed with enough layers for this, but that won't stop me. Knox already has the sled in his hands, and we walk up the hill.

"Okay, you go first." He places the sled on the ground and holds it as I settle, taking a deep breath as it holds my weight. I rush down the hill, laughing, and hit the bottom with a thud.

"That was so much fun," I scream.

"Come back," he calls out, and I meet him at the top.

"Your turn." I place it just how he had before and wait for him to sit.

He shakes his head. "You get on, and I'll climb in after you."

"Are you sure?" I tilt my head. "I'm not sure it'll hold us both." My eyebrows pinch together.

"It will. You rode it perfectly. It's sturdier than I thought," he's so confident.

"Okay." I widen my eyes and pinch my lips. I'm not so sure.

After I sit, Knox gets on behind me—his body close to mine, and his legs caging my sides. I shiver and hold on to the side rails as he pushes us forward. We slide faster than I did on my own. It's a bumpy ride as we reach the bottom, and we land hard, hearing a crack.

"Crap," Knox breathes out, and I turn to see his body is slanted. "I think it broke."

I can't hold in my laughter as I struggle to stand and see part of his behind through the wooden slabs. My entire body shakes with laughter, a cramp striking the side of my rib.

"Very funny. Want to help me up?" He lifts his hand in the air, but I'm clenching my stomach as I laugh.

"Hey!" I screech when he throws a snowball at me.

"I needed to get you to stop laughing and help me," he replies with an excuse.

"You're in no position to start a snowball fight," I threaten.

"Ainsley," he warns as I pack snow in my hands. His eyes widen right before the snowball hits his chin.

He growls and pushes himself up from the ground. I run away from him, remembering the last time we had a snowball fight. When he loops his arm around my waist and lifts me off the ground, he smashes snow in my face.

I yell and try to get away, but his hold is strong. I stop fighting against him and look up into his face as I push snow from my hair. His hand reaches up to swipe some from my shoulder.

"Sorry I broke your sled."

"It's okay," I smile. "It cost like ten bucks, and it was a gamble," I shrug. "At least we had fun."

"That we did." He leans in and kisses the top of my head. "Thank you," he murmurs against my hair.

"For what?" I lean back to look at him.

"For asking me to join you. I know things are a little off after our conversation the other night, but I'm ready to have you in my life."

Before I can argue, he runs his thumb over my lips, and I wait for the kiss. He winks and takes a step back, leaving me wanting to feel his lips against mine. I groan and cross my arms. What a tease.

"Where to now?" he asks.

"I gotta go home and get ready for work. Saturdays are always busy." I wish I could skip work and stay with him here.

"Mind taking me back to my truck?" he asks.

"Not at all. By the way, how many people will be at Thanksgiving dinner?" I give him a sideways glance.

"About fifteen. My aunts and uncles always come to our house."

"Oh, okay," that's a lot more people than I expected.

"Are you nervous?" He gives me a crooked smirk that makes him look like trouble.

"Why would I be?" I cross my arms over my chest, channeling all my confidence. Of course, I'm nervous about meeting his family.

"Because you're going to meet my family," he states.

"So?" I widen my eyes using my best poker face.

"I'm not introducing you as just a new girl in town," he explains.

"Then what are you going to introduce me as?" I raise a brow and challenge, reaching my car.

He places the sled in the trunk and turns to look at me, leaning his hip against the trunk. "As the woman whose heart I'm going to win over." He doesn't hesitate, instead gives me a cocky smile.

"Oh," I say and nod, poker face melting faster than my makeup on a hot Texas day. Okay, well, this Thanksgiving should be interesting. I hop in my car, his response leaving me speechless. He, on the other hand, keeps that grin the entire way back to his car.

chapter 14

Knox

I pull into my parents' house and take in the ranch-style house, the wood siding and stone trimmings around the windows are covered in frost. I rub my hands together and take a deep breath to calm myself from seeing Ainsley earlier. As soon as I caught her by the waist when we were sledding, I wanted to keep her close to my body and get lost in her. I want her to know she's more than just someone to fuck, though.

"Hello," I call out when I walk into the house.

"In here, honey," my mom calls from the kitchen.

"Hi," I kiss her cheek.

"How are you?" She turns to look at me from her position in front of the stove.

"I'm good. How about you guys?" I take a seat at the counter.

"We're good. Preparing for Thanksgiving. You know how your father gets." She shakes her head.

I chuckle. "Yeah. Is he overstocking the bar and wanting to buy three turkeys?" I joke.

"You have no idea." She stands on the other side of the counter, facing me.

"By the way, I don't know if Axel mentioned it, but we invited Ainsley to Thanksgiving. She's new to town and is the bartender at Clarke's. She won't be able to go home and was gonna spend it at home alone," I explain when I should just shut up. Ainsley's rambling is contagious apparently.

"He may have mentioned something." My mom tilts her head and scrutinizes me.

"Okay, good." I nod and slap the countertop. "So, are Dad and Axel outside?"

"They'll be in soon. Why don't you tell me about Ainsley before they walk in." She raises her eyebrows, the hint of a smile on her face.

"What about her?" I shrug.

"She's a nice woman. I personally like her." She surprises me with her declaration.

"You've met her?" My words don't hide the surprise.

"You aren't the only one with a social life, young man. Your father and I go to Clarke's as well. She's very sweet." Her smile gives away what she really thinks, and she's not buying my nonchalant attitude toward Ainsley.

"She is," I nod.

"Well, I hope you give yourself a chance to be happy." She covers my hand with hers. "You deserve it."

"I doubt that, but thanks."

"Hey, we all make mistakes, and we live with the consequences, but we can't let them own us. You want to make a life for yourself after this divorce, then you need to let go of the past. You made choices you weren't proud of, it's how you learn. Bet next time you won't let the woman you love slip from your life." She gives me a pointed look.

"Definitely learned," my tone is flat.

"I do know things happen for a reason. You needed to live that experience and lose someone you cared about, so someone else could enter your life."

I nod, knowing she's right, but it's still a challenge some days. I think about Ainsley and my promise to win her trust. She deserves someone willing to be all in.

"You're here." My father walks into the house through the back porch.

"Got here a few minutes ago. Catching up with Mom." I give him a hug.

"Good, she misses having you around all the time." He points at me as he grabs a bottled water from the fridge.

"I'm here for a long time, now," I assure them.

"Ainsley, Clarke's bartender, will be joining us for Thanksgiving," my mom tells my dad.

"Oh, really? As a friend or a girlfriend?" He looks my way with a knowing laugh.

"Why me? Maybe she's coming with Axel," I defend and they both laugh, shaking their heads. Today was not the day I wanted to tell them about my situation with Ainsley. I promised her I'd introduce her as more than a friend, but I want to make sure she's convinced I mean it.

"Funny," my dad slaps my shoulder. "Your brother isn't interested in her in that way," he confirms.

"We're friends. Axel and I *both* invited her so she wouldn't spend the holiday alone."

"Well, she's more than welcome to spend it with us. No one should spend Thanksgiving alone, especially when they're miles away from family," my dad adds.

"Thanks, I agree." I smile at them, grateful to have my parents in my life for the good and bad.

Axel joins us a few minutes later, passing me a beer while we wait for dinner to be ready.

"Want to go to Clarke's after dinner?" he asks as we sit in the living room, watching a basketball game.

"Sure." I take a chug of my beer. Any excuse to see Ainsley again.

"You got it bad, brother," he laughs.

"Yeah, man." I don't deny it, not with my brother. "She's somethin' else."

"She is, so be good to her," he warns.

I look his way and furrow my eyebrows. "What the hell?"

"I'm just sayin'. I want you to be happy, but it's only fair to her if you're not still holding on to feelings for Reese."

"I'm not." I run a hand down my face. "It's complicated. Reese will always be special, but it's more about the guilt than my actual feelings toward her. I knew we were over the night I saw her, and she told me she was with someone else. She loves him, and I did her wrong." I shake my head.

"Then let it go. Don't hold on to that crap anymore and look at the amazing woman you have in front of you."

"You have a thing for her?" I'm not about to enter some brotherly contest to see which Bentley brother she prefers.

He shakes his head. "Nah, but I care about her as a friend. I know her ex-boyfriend cheated on her, and she doesn't deserve to go through that."

"I'd never cheat. I was loyal to a wife I never loved." I tense in my seat.

"I know, but there are more ways to feel cheated than physical infidelity."

"I get it. If I wasn't ready to move on, I would never have pursued her," I defend my actions.

"I know," he nods, finishing off his beer. "Besides, I think she's perfect for you."

Pensive, I drink my beer. She is perfect for me, in ways I never even thought I'd want in a woman. Her quirkiness draws me in. She's wild and free, yet grounded. I don't know how I'd describe Ainsley, and maybe that's it. I can't find the right words because I've never met anyone like her before.

♪

I end my call with Matt, grateful he checked in to see how I was doing. He asked about Ainsley, and when I told him what was going on, he boasted about how right he was when he visited Everton. It's been two days since I've seen her, and I hope to change that soon.

I scroll through my phone as I sit back on my couch, one leg propped up on the coffee table and crackling of burning wood in the fireplace comforting me. I haven't been on social media much, not wanting to give into the drama of everything that's happened. Taking a break to gather myself means a break from social media as well.

Noticing a few tags in comments on Instagram, I click on the post to see what it's all about.

A baby and a wedding: Reese Stone and Dex Monroe have welcomed their first child, and there's talk of wedding bells in the near future.

I freeze, staring at a photo of Reese with Dex and a newborn. She looks down at the baby with awe, and he's staring at her with so damn much love.

I blow out a heavy breath and smile. She looks happy, happier than I've ever seen her. The next photo on the post is one of Dex and Reese looking at each other. At one point in time, I thought she and I would share photos like these, but the only thing running through my mind is how happy I am that she found that with someone like Dex. From what I hear, he's a great guy. I had to ask around when she first told me she was seeing him. I had no right, but the protectiveness I carried when it came to Reese took over.

I don't bother reading the comments I'm tagged in, knowing it isn't worth the stress or taking away from their moment. I wish them the best, and I feel proud for having known her and been a part of her life. I close my eyes, only one smiling face appearing behind my eyelids, and she's blonde not brunette.

I type on my phone, smiling to myself.

KnoxBentleyOfficial: hey, I hear there's a gangster and beautiful woman who owns this account. She also loves Frito pie and rapping to

Eminem after she goes sledding on antique sleds. Just so happens this woman sounds perfect

While I wait for her to reply, I grab a beer from my fridge and sit back on the couch, scrolling through the television channels. After a few minutes, I check my phone, noticing she read the message, but she hasn't replied. I exhale and wait a few more minutes. Maybe she went into work a little earlier today. I look again, and still no message or bubbles showing she's typing.

Crap. I don't know how else to prove to her that I'm ready to have her in my life.

When she doesn't answer after thirty minutes, I figure she's busy at work, and I make a plan to go to Clarke's later tonight to see her.

I drop my beer bottle in the recycling bin and stare out the glass doors, watching the light snow falling onto my yard. I stretch my arms over my head, gripping the door frame to stretch and look over my shoulder when I hear a knock on the door. Guessing it's Axel, I walk to the door and open without checking.

"Hey." Doe eyes look at me while teeth puncture her bottom lip.

A slow smile creeps on my face. "Hi." I reach for her and pull her into a hug, inhaling her flowery scent and the cold around her. I close the door, keeping my arm around her. When her arms loop around my body, I feel like a lucky bastard.

"What are you doing here?" I look down at her. "Not that I'm complaining, but I was waiting for you to respond to my message."

Ainsley takes a step back and shrugs. "I saw the news and wanted to make sure you were doing okay." Her expression doesn't change, full lips set in a straight line and eyes still wide as they look up at me.

I tilt my head and grab the back of my neck. "I'm doing fuckin' fantastic," I tell her with honesty. "I've told you, she's not my present or my future. What I had to do to her was hard, and I hate myself because I've never been the guy to cause pain, but she's not the woman I want to be showing up on my doorstep unannounced."

"Really?"

Using my thumb, I remove her bottom lip from her teeth and nod. "I promise. I read the post, and my reaction was pride and happiness for them. She deserves to be happy, especially with a good guy. Maybe at one time, I wanted that with her, but that's changed." I put my heart out there, hoping she'll catch it. I'm not sure I can handle it shattering again.

"I just don't want to push more than you're ready for."

"Push, babe, push as hard as you can," my words rush out.

"Are you sure? Because I'm pretty strong." Her eyebrows pop up and she flexes her arm, showing me her muscles.

My head falls back as I laugh. "You are strong," the meaning double.

I pull her to me by the waist and keep my hands there. "I know my life's been a shit show for the last few years, and for all I know I'll be poor in the next few years and have to beg my dad to give me a job at the ranch, but what I know for certain is that I want to spend time with you. I want you in my life, as more than a friend." I kiss her forehead.

"I want Frito pie nights and tubing dates. I want you to sing my songs instead of Eminem's," I smirk. "Give me a chance?" I ask.

She nods and wraps her arms around my neck. "How can I say no to that?" Her lips land on mine as if it's the most natural thing in the world. I pull her closer to me, deepening the kiss, wanting more than a few innocent pecks.

I lift her, and she wraps her legs around me, laughing as I walk us into the living room and set her on the couch. "I'm going to add more wood to the fireplace," I whisper over her lips.

Ainsley tucks her legs under her as she watches me stoke the fireplace.

"Do you have to go to work?" I turn to look at her, standing from my position in front of the fireplace.

"I had swapped shifts with Adam today and worked the morning," she explains.

"So that means you have the evening free?" I stalk toward her, smirking.

"Yup," she nods, raising an eyebrow.

"Great. What do you want to drink?" I rub my hands together, the warmth of the fireplace filling the room.

"Scotch," she winks, and I chuckle.

Serving us both a glass, I join her on the couch and tap her glass with mine. "Cheers."

"Cheers," she echoes and sips her drink.

"My mom's excited you'll be joining us for Thanksgiving," I tell her.

"Are you sure it's okay?" She shifts on the couch to angle her body toward me.

"Of course, my parents both agreed. No one should spend this holiday alone. I wouldn't allow it."

"Allow it?" Her eyes pop open, and her eyebrows lift on her forehead, causing me to laugh. "Newsflash, buddy, I'm my own boss." She jabs a finger against my chest.

"I know." I grab her hand and bring her toward me. "But I wouldn't let you spend the day by yourself. I'd have gone to your place and made sure you had someone that cared about you with you."

"That's really sweet." Her eyes soften, and she smiles before kissing my cheek.

"Now…" I let the word linger, collecting my thoughts. "I want to introduce you as my girlfriend, not Ainsley, Clarke's bartender, or a friend."

She runs her hand through her hair, flipping it to a side, "Are you sure?"

"Positive," I reassure her.

chapter 15

Knox

I've spent as much time as I could with Ainsley these last few days, from lunch dates at her place where we make Frito pie to secret flirting while she's at work. She doesn't know this yet, but I've even picked up my guitar a few times and strummed some chords, remembering what it's like to play without the pressure of dollar signs.

Tonight will mark a new step in our relationship. Up until now, only my parents and Axel know about my relationship with Ainsley, but the rest of my family will meet her soon when we get to my parents' house for Thanksgiving dinner. As much as I can ask them to keep this quiet for now, it's hard to control what will happen.

Ready to introduce her to everyone and spend the evening with her, I jump out of my truck and put on my coat before making my way to her apartment door. I rub my hands and blow into them while I wait for her to answer.

"Hey," her bright smile greets me.

I pause, looking her up and down. "Hi," I grin, walking into her apartment and kissing her.

"Well, I like that greeting," she teases as my arms remain loosely around her waist. "Do I look okay?" She looks down between us.

"You look beautiful," I state.

"I can change if it's too much or too casual," she rambles.

"I said you look beautiful," I interrupt her. "Gorgeous." I kiss her soft lips.

"Don't ruin my makeup," she chastises.

"I plan to ruin it later," I wink and hold her hand, taking her in—ivory sweater, short camel skirt with buttons down the front that gives me ideas that aren't appropriate for a family dinner, and black tights with black booties. When I look at her face again, I see her red lipstick is smudged. I chuckle, reaching out and running my thumb along the edge of her lips to wipe away the bit that spread.

Ainsley laughs, and I furrow my eyebrows. "Your lips are red," she blushes, wiping her thumb across my lips. I nip the pad of her finger, and she raises her brow, looking into my eyes with mischief. "Behave," she pats my chest. "You look handsome." She steps back and does her own assessment of my outfit.

"Babe, we better go before we skip dinner altogether," I warn.

"You hittin' on me, Mr. Bentley?" She shimmies and winks.

I groan, watching her body move.

Ainsley's laughter carries her into the kitchen, and she reappears with a wrapped pie dish.

"I'll take that." I grab it from her.

"Thanks. Let me just put on my coat, and we can head out. I'm nervous," she confesses.

"You have no reason to be, trust me." I drop a kiss on her temple as she puts on her coat and then wraps a plaid scarf around her neck.

After a deep breath, Ainsley looks at me. "Okay, let's do this." She claps her hands quickly.

"Come on." I lace our fingers, holding the pie with my other hand, and lead us to my truck.

"Oh, my God!" She grips my hand as she slips on a patch of ice, shaking me as well.

"The pie?" She looks at me with wide eyes.

"It's in one piece," I assure her, trying not to chuckle at her freaked-out expression.

"Phew. Okay, let's make it to your car without any mishaps." Her chest slowly rises and falls as she attempts to calm her nerves.

"Ainsley, relax. You've already met my parents and the rest of my family is easy going."

"Yeah, but I met them as Ainsley, your bartender for the night, *not* Ainsley, your son's girlfriend," she says in a deep voice.

"Are you mocking me?" I ask as I hold the door open for her, cocking my head to the side.

"I'm mocking myself. I'm not sure why I deepened my voice," she giggles.

I shake my head and kiss her. Taking the pie from my hands, she places it on her lap, and I make my way around my truck, ready to introduce her to everyone.

"So, you said your aunts and uncles would be here, your cousins, and who else?" Ainsley asks as I drive.

"That's all. My mom's brother and his wife, their daughter, and then my dad's sister and brother with their spouses and two of my cousins on that side. I'm not sure if any of them have girlfriends at the moment. I do have another cousin that spends Thanksgiving with his wife and her family in Virginia." I give her the spark notes version of my family.

"That's not too bad," she whispers to herself.

I reach for her hand, weaving our fingers together. I never expected to meet a woman like her. When I thought everything in my life was ruined, she smiled my way and sparked hope. I've wanted to know her since that night at Clarke's, and that morning I ran into her at the coffee shop where she was checking her mail and asking if I wanted to sit with her. This woman is fearless but vulnerable, and she's teaching me both of those things can coexist.

When her other hand covers our linked fingers, a feeling of protection comes over me. I want to take care of this woman, but she's also doing that to me. She doesn't fault me for my past mistakes, and her gentle touch shows me she likes me just as I am, no fame or career, simply Knox Bentley, Wyoming native that loves snow, horses, and his family.

I'm fucking fortunate to have found a woman like her because she's a rare one. Ainsley rushed to my house to comfort me, thinking I'd be in a bad place when she read Reese had a baby, not knowing that the only woman I wanted was her. She selflessly put her feelings aside to take care of me.

I lift our tangled fingers and kiss the top of her hand. "Thank you for being with me," I sneak a glance her way.

"You're welcome," her words come out slowly, unsure.

"I'm lucky to have you in my life, and I haven't told you that."

Her mouth splits into a wide smile. "You're something else, Knox." Her head leans back, and her eyes close, but the smile is permanent. She rolls her head against the headrest and looks at me, the corner of my eyes flick toward her periodically.

"You starin'?" I ask, my voice light.

"Shhh… Don't interrupt me," she teases. Her fingers follow the lines of my profile and feel my beard. When they reach the side of my lips, I turn my head, eyes still on the road, and kiss her fingertips.

"Ready?" I ask then, pulling into the ranch.

"Yes," she sighs, much more relaxed than when I got to her house.

I open the front door, and chatter hits us. Ainsley squeezes the hand she's holding, and I look at her, winking. She smiles, leaning her head on my shoulder, as we make our way into the house.

"You're here," my mom beams, walking toward us. "Hi, Ainsley, I'm so glad you're joining us." She pulls Ainsley by the shoulders and wraps her arms around her. I chuckle at her excitement.

"Thank you for having me, Mrs. Bentley." She smiles at my mom, calm and confident like the woman I've come to know.

"It's our pleasure, and please, call me Deb." My mom looks at me and wraps her arms around me, almost knocking the pie I'm holding.

"Hi, Mom," I laugh.

"Come in. Knox, you can introduce Ainsley to everyone," she says as she takes the pie from my hand. "Thank you for making this," she directs her attention to Ainsley.

"You're welcome. I love pumpkin pie, and I make it every year." Ainsley doesn't skip a beat.

"Hi, Ainsley, it's nice to see you," my dad joins my mom. "And before you call me Mr. Bentley, please call me Dean."

"It's nice to see you again," she smirks.

As we walk further into the kitchen, I introduce her to everyone. If I guessed, I'd say my mom already gave them a warning before I arrived. No one seems to be surprised by my arrival with Ainsley.

"How does it feel to be back livin' here?" Uncle Ben, my mom's brother, asks after Ainsley, and I take a seat at the dining room table.

"It's been good," I nod. "Missed being here." I take a sip of scotch, relaxing as the amber liquid warms me.

"Cheers to that." He holds his glass up, tapping mine. "How are you liking Everton?" he asks Ainsley.

"I love it." Her face lights up. "It's colder than I'm used to, but the town is great, and I love the mountains here." She runs two fingers up and down the stem of her wineglass, but otherwise, she seems relaxed.

"How long have you been living here for?" Lily, my cousin, asks.

"Not too long, a few months. I lived in Colorado before, just outside of Denver."

"That's cool. Are you from Colorado?" Lily smiles, tilting her head a bit. My little cousin is anything but subtle, and her curiosity is painted on her face.

Ainsley leans back into the chair, now holding the wine glass. "I'm actually from Texas, but I was relocated to Colorado with my previous employer. I recently realized my job wasn't satisfying me the way it used to, and I felt like I needed a change, so here I am. I bartend at Clarke's in the evenings, wasting away my college degree, but I've never been happier." She lets it all out and takes a sip of wine. I hold in my laughter.

"That's brave. I don't think that I could move somewhere I'd never been before," Lily raises her eyebrows as she thinks about it.

"You went to Arizona for college," I remind her.

"Yeah, but college is different. You're going, knowing you'll make friends and have some kind of plan," she shrugs.

"Do you still live there?" Ainsley asks her.

"Yes, I'm a Senior."

"That's exciting." I watch the interaction between the two, leaning back and crossing my ankle over my leg. I catch Ben's eye, and he nods with a smile.

As the rest of my family arrives, I introduce them to Ainsley, my aunts and uncles curious about her and our relationship. My guess is my mom didn't have a chance to talk to her in-laws beforehand.

"We missed you last Thanksgiving," Aunt Charlotte, my dad's sister, says as she sits with us, her own wineglass in hand.

"Yeah," I nod. "Hopefully I'll be around for a lot more from now on." I leave it at that.

"Yes." She reaches out and pats my hand. "You look good," she whispers.

"Thanks." I nod, knowing the main reason I feel the way I do has to do with the woman beside me, spending time with my family as if she's known them for years. Amelia never cared to get to know my family. In fact, she refused to spend time with them, making me come to Wyoming on my own whenever I'd visit.

"Hey, Ainsley." She turns around to look at Axel, who's calling out to her from the living room. "Your Cowboys are getting a whipping," he laughs.

"They are not." She crosses her arms and glares at him.

"They're goin' down," he teases her.

She turns to look at me with a serious expression. "I'll be right back." Her hand lands on my forearm, and it makes me fucking proud that she's mine. I nod and watch her go. For Axel's sake, I hope he's right.

"I like her," Lily leans forward on the table and whispers, her eyes staring at the living room. "She seems really nice."

Amused by her attempt at being subtle, I tell her, "She's great. Glad you like her."

"Much better than you know who." Her eyes widen and roll.

"Yeah." I nod. Lily has never been good at hiding her feelings, less so with Amelia.

"Hey, I didn't mean to upset you."

"Trust me, you didn't. My divorce was a long time coming," I share, pursing my lips.

"I never did understand that relationship." She taps her fingertips together.

I shake my head and shrug, not knowing what to say. I'm tired of giving her excuses for my connection to Amelia. Lily isn't stupid. She grew up with Axel and me, and she knows I'd never really go for a woman like Amelia.

"I know, I know. I'll drop it." She falls back on her chair, crossing her arms, and exhaling, her lips vibrating. I laugh at the sound and shake my head.

"Brat," I mock.

"That's what happens when you're the youngest in the family *and* the only girl," she smiles with confidence, batting her eyelashes.

"Oh!" A loud scream echoes around the house, and I shoot up to my feet as my head whips to the living room.

"Be back." I look at everyone sitting at the table and stalk over to where Axel and Ainsley are. "Is everything okay?" I see Axel cheering and Ainsley staring at the television, her arms crossed and body tense.

My shoulders shake in silent laughter, and I walk up to her, wrapping my arms around her.

"Jesus," she shrieks. I let out a loud laugh, and she hits my arm. "You scared the heck out of me."

"Sorry," I whisper in her ear, causing her to shiver.

She leans back, allowing me to support her, and watches the game. "If we lose, Axel will never let me live this down," she murmurs.

"Damn straight." He hears her despite her attempt at being discreet.

"I can't stand the Patriots," she confides.

"I'm indifferent," I shrug. "Football's not my thing."

"No?" She turns around in my arms, "What is?"

"Basketball." I tighten my arms around her.

"I don't really follow it," she purses her lips.

"All right, y'all are boring me. Be back when the game starts up again," Axel interrupts us, and I realize there's a commercial break.

I look down at Ainsley and wink. "I thought he'd never leave."

Her body shakes with laughter. "You're mean."

"Nah, I just wanted to be alone with you." I kiss her plump lips.

"Can we take a picture?" She wears a crooked smirk and hopeful eyes.

"Of course." I pull my phone from my pocket and hold it up, facing us. "Say cheese," I whisper in her ear. Ainsley turns to kiss my cheek just as I snap the photo. I click on the picture to look at how it turned out. It's blurry from her movement, but I can't help but smile at it.

"Let's take another one. Promise not to move this time." She crinkles her nose before her mouth splits into a smile.

"Ready?" I ask and snap the picture.

"Much better," she says as I open it up so we can see it. "Send it to me." I squirm when Ainsley squeezes my ribs. "Are you ticklish?" She squints her eyes deviously.

"No," I warn.

"Okay, I'll be nice." She winks, and I groan. I want to take her home, kiss her everywhere, and then feel her wrapped around me.

I take a deep breath and adjust myself.

"Are you having naughty thoughts?" She leans up on her toes and whispers in my ear, her soft breath against the shell of my ear, not helping the situation.

"You have no idea," I clutch her hip.

"Me too," she confesses and waggles her eyebrows.

"Babe, you gotta stop. We have to get through dinner, dessert, and more drinks before I can take you home."

"Mmm… I'll be good." Ainsley takes a step backward, shaking her body.

"Come 'ere," I beckon her with my finger.

"Oh yeah?" She dances toward me without music. Laughter moves through my body as I watch her.

"Yeah," I sigh. When she's close enough, I pull her to me and kiss the top of her head. "You're something else."

"I'll take that as a compliment."

"Trust me, it's the best kind." I stare into her eyes, holding her face. My lips brush against hers right before my mom calls everyone to dinner. "Let's get this party going so we can go home," I whisper over her lips. Her quiet moan tells me she's feeling the same thing as me.

Chapter 16

Ainsley

I sigh in contentment as I close my eyes while Knox drives. I hear his soft chuckle and smile to myself. "Are you laughing at me?" I ask, my eyes still closed and hand patting my stomach in satisfaction. The Bentley's know how to host Thanksgiving.

I loved his family. They were so kind, and no one made me feel unwelcome, despite his recent divorce.

"A little bit," his deep voice moves over me.

"Well, stop."

"Nah." I feel his hand land on my thigh. All night I've been wanting to be close to him, touch him, feel his arms around me.

"You'll pay for that," I threaten him.

"Oh, I'm looking forward to it."

I peak one eye open and look at him. "You'll be sorry you encouraged me," I tease. I really have no idea how I'd make him pay, although a few ideas cross my mind. I shiver at the possibilities.

"Are you having naughty thoughts," he repeats my question from earlier.

"Mmm... Maybe."

"Good." He grips my thigh, and I inhale sharply through my lips. I feel it everywhere in my body, needing more.

I turn my head to face him and hold his hand. "Want to stay at my place?" I pinch my lips to the side as I wait for his reply.

"You sure?" He glances my way quickly.

"Yeah." I lift his hand and kiss the top of it. I'm ready to take this step with him.

"I'd love to." He winks in my direction, thumb rubbing my palm.

As soon as we get home, I walk carefully to the entrance of my apartment building, making sure I don't slip this time. Once we're inside, Knox's hands are on my hips, his lips kissing the back of my neck. When he pulls me back to his body, I moan at the feel of his erection on my lower back.

"Babe," he whispers. "Thank you for tonight."

"I had fun." I bite down another moan and turn to face him. My arms fall lazily around his neck. "I really like you, and I'm glad I got to meet your family. I know this is new, and you could've just introduced me as a friend, but I'm grateful you didn't."

"No," he shakes his head. "I won't hide you." His face grows serious. "I hope you understand that." I run my fingers across his forehead, smoothing out his pinched eyebrows.

"Thank you," I whisper before leaning up on my toes and kissing him.

Knox groans into my mouth and walks us further into my apartment, my back hitting the wall with his body caging me. His tongue sweeps along mine, his teeth nipping my lower lip, and his hands traveling up and down my body.

I push forward, melting against him as my fingers tangle in the longer curls on the nape of his neck. Knox rounds his hands over my butt and picks me up. I tug his hair and kiss him desperately as I feel the hardness in his jeans hitting my core against the thin material of my tights.

"Knox," I moan, tilting my head back, and giving him access to kiss my neck and base of my throat. My nipples harden, and every sensation I feel as he rubs against my body on his way to my bedroom intensifies the desire I'm feeling.

Once in my room, he drops me on the bed and kneels before me. He gives me a heady kiss, tongue peeking out, before moving back on his haunches and looking me up and down with hunger. Wordlessly, he removes my booties. Knox's hands skim up and down my legs in appreciation before sneaking under my skirt and finding the waistband of my tights. I lift my body to encourage him so he can pull them down slowly, his calloused fingers heating the skin he's exposing.

Our eyes lock in a heated gaze, and we remain silent as we let our bodies communicate. Knox's fingers graze my calves, making me break out in goosebumps. He drops a kiss on my thigh and stands, leaning his body over me. I push back and catch his lips with mine. The weight of his body is a welcomed pressure as my legs fall open so he can fit between them.

Our kisses are fervent and chaotic, hands moving everywhere and struggling to reach the places we want. I sneak my hands underneath his sweater and tug the hem, tearing it up off his body. Before he has a chance to lean back down, I reach for the buttons on his Oxford shirt and quickly undo them. When I reach the last one, Knox stills my hands with his. His shirt falls open, his broad chest peppered with hair and his defined stomach causing me to clench my thighs.

Knox grabs my wrists and places my hands over my head. "Keep them there," his hoarse voice fills the quiet of my bedroom, interrupting the silence. I simply nod and look on to see what his next move is.

Once again, his hands land on my legs, moving up and down my skin as his opened shirt tickles me. They travel up my body, inching my sweater up my torso and stopping right under my breasts. I sigh with exasperation, and his eyes fill with mischievous laughter. The pads of his fingertips trace the edge of the sweater, brushing against the underside of my breasts.

"My goodness." I close my eyes, my heart picking up speed.

"You like that?" He leans down to kiss me, the pressure against my core causing me to moan and arch my body. "I'll take that as a yes."

"Knox... Come on," I urge him.

"Uh-uh. Keep your hands up there." He points to my arms that are mid-air on the way to his body.

I clench the pillow above my head and lift my lower body to touch his. His eyes travel down to where I'm moving and are set alight.

"I want that, too, but with due time," he whispers as if we're in a forbidden rendezvous. In a way, it feels that way. Me in bed with Knox Bentley, talented musician. He's more than that, though. He's kind, funny, broody, unique.

The tension in my body relaxes as I take in the man I'm sure the public doesn't know. How lucky am I? Against his argument, I move one of my hands to reach up and touch his face. He closes his eyes and leans into my touch.

"I want to remember this," I say softly.

"Me too." He shifts his head to kiss my palm before returning it to its place above my head. "You're beautiful." He drops his head and kisses my stomach.

Knox finally removes my sweater, following a trail of kisses up my stomach to the swell of my breasts and up my neck, gentle bites alternating with his kisses.

His beard tickles my skin, adding to the sensations covering my body like a lust-filled blanket. When his hand sneaks behind my back, I arch so he can reach his destination. With my bra undone, he removes it and takes me in. His eyes linger on my breasts, a wicked smile painting his face.

"Stunning." His kiss comes in fast and deep, his calloused fingers moving between us as they pinch my nipples. I cry out, needing to feel more. He takes my reaction as a green light to continue palming my breasts and twisting my nipples, shooting desire straight to my core. My breathing comes in more rapid and shallow, his lips and hands the cause of it.

Unable to hold back, I reach for him, running my hands up his chest and unhooking his shirt from his shoulders. He breaks away from me a second so I can finish removing it, and he's back on me, his lips claiming me.

Knox groans when my nails run down his back, feeling his muscles flex. "I want to take my time, but fuck, you feel good."

"Let's throw expectations and time out the window. Touch me, kiss me, do whatever you want. Right now, I'm all yours," I surrender to him on my bed, watching and waiting.

"Ainsley," he breathes my name. His hands skim from my breasts to the top of my skirt, lifting part of his body so he can reach better. He looks up at me, asking for permission and I nod.

He undoes the brass buttons on the front of my skirt until it's open enough for him to slide it down my legs. Knox steps off the bed, tugging his hair and staring at me in only my underwear.

"Take off your jeans," I demand.

His eyes meet mine again, and he smirks. "Bossy."

His hands remove his belt and unsnap the button. Slowly, he teases me with lowering the zipper. When his jeans drop to the floor, I take in his almost naked body.

"Boxer briefs," I add with a quirk of my eyebrow.

"Nuh-uh, you have to remove your underwear, too."

I kneel on the bed, holding his stare, as I hook my fingers inside my thong and remove it. Once it's off, I lean back on the bed, holding my body up with my elbows and raise my eyebrows.

That sexy smirk is back on his face. He takes off his boxer briefs and wraps his hand around his cock, slowly moving it up and down.

"Holy shit." The words escape my mouth on a gasp before I can rein them in, and I feel warmth fill my cheeks. Knox chuckles as he crawls back onto the bed. His lips land on the crook of my neck, and his fingers touch where I need him. I tense as he brushes a finger over my clit, moaning at the sensation.

"You're so wet," he murmurs against my skin. I nod, silent.

Knox works my body, fingers entering me, lips marking me, and heart owning me. My body wriggles and tenses underneath his when his fingers curl inside me, hitting that spot that makes me come undone. He takes my reaction as encouragement and continues to thrust his fingers, his thumb pressing down on my clit. I cry out, moving my hand down his body and wrapping it around his length. I stroke his cock, adding pressure, and he grunts.

My head lifts, kissing his neck before sucking his earlobe between my teeth and Knox hisses. He adds pressure to my pussy, his fingers rubbing that perfect spot. Panting, I gasp for air as my toes curl.

"Oh, my God," I call out.

"I want to see you come undone," Knox growls. "I want to be the reason you moan." He kisses me.

My body trembles, heat rising from the base of my spine, covering me. He pinches my nipple with his free hand, and I reach for the other one with mine, while I continue to jerk him.

"That's fucking hot." His voice is husky, heavy with desire. "I need you to stop moving your hand, or I'm going to come, and I quite frankly prefer to come inside of you." I remove my hand from around his cock and arch my body, my orgasm taking over as I call out his name on repeat.

"You're gorgeous when you fall apart." He gives me a closed-mouth kiss. Spent, I catch my breath as I watch him reach for a condom in his jeans. "Are you sure you're ready for all of this?" He holds up the condom.

"Yes." I reach my hand out for him, prepared to share this moment with him.

Knox joins me on the bed and rolls the condom down his length. I watch as he positions himself over me, widening my legs. He rolls his hips, entering me slowly, giving me time to adjust.

"Are you okay?"

"Mmhh," I swallow a moan. "More than," the words get caught in my throat.

Knox enters me completely, kissing me gently as we connect as intimately as two people can. I get lost in his body, the feel of his arms holding me, his kisses, tender and greedy all at once. The sensation of having him inside of me, this moment is a memory I'll have seared in my heart for the rest of my life.

A burst of feeling explodes all around me as we begin to move together, faster, both of us chasing our climax. I wrap my legs around Knox's waist, bringing him deeper, and dig my nails into his back. A silent orgasm rises in me, muting my moans as my body bows off the mattress. My heels dig into Knox's backside, hoping to God he continues to thrust inside of me as I ride out this wave.

His lips crash onto mine, his hips speeding up as he groans, his own orgasm meeting mine. Our bodies tense and our moans fill the space in my bedroom. My core pulses around him as the pleasure intensifies and chills kiss my skin. Knox growls as he thrusts deeper, harder, before stilling inside of me.

Breathless, he drops his head on my shoulder, holding me before pulling out. A kiss falls on my collarbone, then his eyes meet mine.

"Amazing," is all he says. I look into the swirls of brown with tiny golden specks as I grin. I brush a few curls from his face. My goodness, that was more than amazing. Connecting with him in this way has my heart thrumming in my chest. I look at the man before me, wondering how I ever thought I could keep things platonic between us.

After we each use the bathroom, we lie in bed. Knox wraps his arms around my waist, my back against his front. "It's been a very long time since I've felt this way."

His breath tickles my ear. I turn around to face him, holding his face.

"Me too. If I'm being completely honest, I don't know that I've ever felt this way." The emotions when I'm with him are new, different. Maybe it has to do that in the last few months I've thrown caution to the wind and lived a life I've wanted to chase for a long time. Maybe I don't feel like the pressure of my career is molding me into a version of myself that wasn't authentic. With Knox, I've been myself from the beginning, quirky and carefree. I haven't cared if he liked me or not, he just simply did. There's nothing more liberating than being who you are without judgment or feeling a need to impress someone.

His breath fans across my face before he drops a kiss on my lips. "The man in me makes me proud to hear that, knowing I made you feel that way."

I cuddle into him, hugging his body to mine and sneaking one of my legs between his, so we're tangled together. Knox chuckles but tightens his hold on me.

Going to sleep in Knox's arms, wrapped up in his warmth, I couldn't think of a better way to end this night.

"Goodnight," I whisper.

"Goodnight, babe." Knox kisses the crown of my head.

chapter 17

Knox

I tug Ainsley's hand so she stops walking and bring her closer to me. I watch her smile shine and drop my free hand to her waist. These last couple of weeks have been heaven with Ainsley by my side. When she's not at work, she's with me. Making me laugh, live, and appreciate the things I've turned a blind eye to.

I inch closer, dropping my lips to hers and pausing right before I kiss her.

"People are looking," she murmurs, her breath teasing my lips.

"I don't care." People in town have already started scrutinizing about our relationship. The rumor-mill already began, and I don't give a shit what they say so long as they don't hurt Ainsley.

"What if…" she trails off, looking around us.

I hold her face and turn it back to mine, so her eyes are on me when I say, "I don't care what they say or think. If they hurt you or mess with you, I'll kill them, but I'm not hiding my feelings for you."

"You'd kill them?" Her eyebrows pinch together, and the ghost of a smile appears on her full lips. My eyes drop to her mouth and back up to her eyes.

"I'm not a violent man, but if anyone tries to hurt you, I will do something about it."

"That's oddly romantic and very hot." Her eyebrows dance on her forehead.

I release her face and place my hands on her hips, adding pressure. She squirms, and I wink.

"Tease," she challenges me.

"You know I never tease without following through." I inch closer to her so she can feel my dick against her.

"We're not done Christmas shopping," she states, blinking up at me.

"We can finish tomorrow," I suggest.

Ainsley shakes her head as she gives me a lopsided smile. "Nope. It's my day off." She grabs hold of one of my hands and moves away, leading the way to the next store. I groan, and my dick argues with her decision, but I let her guide me. This woman is making me believe in life again. The simple joys I hadn't experienced in years are now back in full-force.

By the time we've finished, we've each gotten the gifts we need. I protested when she grabbed presents for my parents and brother, assuring her she didn't need to, but she insisted she wanted to. The only gift I have left to buy is hers, but I want it to be a surprise.

"Want to grab dinner?" I turn to look at her as the streetlights illuminate the sidewalk.

"Yes, I'm starving." She tilts her head back as if thinking of a place. "Want Italian?"

"Works for me." We walk to the one Italian restaurant in town and wait a few minutes for a table.

"People are staring," Ainsley says as she leans into my side.

"So?" I look down at her. She shrugs and keeps observing the place.

"I just… I don't know. We haven't really talked about 'going public'," she uses air quotes.

"Right now, I'm Knox Bentley, born and raised Everton resident. My career is on hold, and so is my image."

Ainsley looks up at me, her eyes are slits. "Your image is never on pause. You're too big to go unnoticed. People are curious about your divorce, your break from music, what's coming next. We can't ignore this." She shakes her head, her lips set in a straight line.

"I know we can't, but can we talk about it later?" I plead, pinching her waist.

"Yeah." She nods, eyes shifting to the side so she can look at the peering faces.

"Ainsley, I want to be with you. Nothing else matters to me. Like I said, unless they interfere in your life, they can say what they want about me. You and I both know the truth." I widen my eyes with deep meaning as I stare into hers.

"I know that. However, I don't want you to go through more crap than you have." Her arms wrap around my body protectively, and I relax. I fucking love having her nestled next to me.

"I appreciate that." I lean down and kiss her when I hear a throat being cleared near us. I look up to find the hostess.

"Your table is ready," she tries a grin for a measure, but it's forced.

"Thanks." I follow her, Ainsley's hand in mine, in case anyone was unsure about our relationship. I'm staking my claim and sending a message, this woman is mine, and I'll protect what we have. I've learned from my prior actions, and I won't let fear or uncertainty break up the best thing in my life.

"Have you given thought to what Harris suggested?" Ainsley asks as she swallows a bite of her lasagna.

"No. I'll worry about that after the holidays. I haven't spent the holidays here in two years, and I want to enjoy it." Harris called earlier this week, bringing up the idea of creating our own label again. Except, this time he proposed that instead of me performing and recording, we sign on an artist and I work the business aspect until I decide if I want to go back to singing. The details were appealing, I won't lie, but at the moment I want to take things slow. Besides, starting a label is a lot of work. It doesn't matter how many contacts I have, the industry is competitive, and I'd be starting from scratch after my break from RWB Records.

"That's smart. Take your time. I'll support whatever decision you make."

I smile. "I don't deserve you."

"Hey," Ainsley frowns and her eyebrows knit together. "That's not true." She shakes her head.

"You're good," I claim.

"So are you." She reaches across the table and holds my hand. I inhale the comfort in her touch.

"Are you done?" I ask. When Ainsley nods, I flag down our waiter and pay.

"Let's go for a drive," I tell her on the way back to my truck.

Ainsley doesn't bother sitting by the door, automatically sitting in the center of the cab bench. I like that she isn't shy about showing her feelings. I like a whole lot about her—her laugh, her confidence, the way she cares for me.

The town's taken notice in our relationship these last few weeks, but I've yet to see anything made public. I want to protect her as much as possible, but I know it's inevitable. Soon, we'll be shared with millions of people. Our privacy and intimacy will be disturbed, and that thought makes me angry. We're safe in our bubble, but it's only a matter of time before the paps come and see what I'm up to, or someone around here posts a picture of the two of us for the media to have a field day with.

I should be the first to share the news, but I'll want to talk to her about it first.

"Where to?" she asks as her land lazily runs circles on my thigh. My muscles twitch, and my dick wants to make itself noticed.

"Let's see where the road leads," I wink. Driving in the open has always been liberating. It helps clear my mind, but it also gives us time away from the rest of the world.

"Can I turn on the radio?" she asks. She knows I keep it off most times, disconnecting from it all.

"Go for it."

She leans forward, turning the dial so we can hear the music before she changes stations. After a few minutes, she decides on what she wants to listen to, and I chuckle. She sings next to me, swaying to the words of Keith Urban. Her lips continue to murmur as she places her head on my shoulder, and I guide us through the winding road.

I slow down and dim the lights. "What's going on?" She leans up and peers out the window.

"Wild horses," I whisper as if any noise would scare them off.

"Where?" She leans forward, and I point to the barely visible animals.

"By those trees." I turn on my fog lights, hoping they stay where they are.

"Oh, wow." Her eyes widen like a small child. "So pretty," she sighs.

"Yeah." I squeeze her thigh and kiss her temple. "I love the wilderness here." We watch them a few more minutes, and then I drive slowly not to disturb them. One of the horses looks our way as we pass it, but it remains still.

I stop the car in a clearing a couple miles away and put it in park. Everything around us is covered in snow. I bring Ainsley to my lap and kiss her, my fingers tangling in her hair.

"Do you want to come with me to Nashville for New Year's Eve?" I ask as I bring my lips to her neck, sucking her skin.

"Mmmm…" she moans and leans back. "Is that a good idea?" She runs her hand through my beard, and I close my eyes.

"Very good idea," my voice is deep.

"Knox," she says sternly. I open my eyes to look at her.

"Hmm?" A slow smile tilts my lips up.

"Nashville?" She raises her eyebrows and pops her eyes open, jerking her head.

"Come with me." I run my hands down the sides of her body and cup her ass, wishing she was straddling me.

"I can't talk to you about this when you're touching me," she deadpans.

"Am I distracting you?" I lift a brow.

"Yes." She tries to cross her arms, but I grab hold of them and intertwine our fingers together. She sighs and looks at me. "Everyone will be there, and then people will know you're dating someone for sure."

"Good, they should know. I'm not ashamed of it." I clench my jaw.

Her hands release mine and come to my face, gently massaging my cheeks. "I don't know if I'll be able to take the night off from work, but I'll ask."

I kiss her, thrusting my tongue into her mouth, seeking hers. She melts against me, returning the kiss just as fiercely.

"Do you want to say you're with someone?" she whispers against my mouth.

"Yes. I want people to know I'm with you, out in the open without either of us looking over our shoulder. I want to show the world the amazing woman I've met, the woman who's inspired me." I hug her to me, kissing the top of her head.

"I mean when you put it that way," she teases, and I hear the smile in her voice.

"Come with me," I plead.

"I'll ask Adam if I can get those days off because I'm assuming we won't be back until the first."

"Probably, if not, we can fly back after midnight. Although, having you to myself to kick off the new year would be perfect." I drop a kiss on her lips.

"That does sound nice. Still, are you sure you think it's a good idea for me to go with you?" She bites her lower lip.

"I've never been more certain. Trust me." I lean back and stare at her face, taking her in. "I don't want anyone else but you."

She breathes out of her mouth, and her body relaxes.

"Let's go home." I lean into her ear and suck on her lobe. "I've got plans for us."

"I won't argue with that." Her voice is husky as she slides onto the seat and buckles up. I chuckle at her enthusiasm and take us back to my place, ready to taste her body until she's begging me to stop.

We're taking our time to get to know each other, but no matter the speed we've tried to control when it comes to our relationship, my feelings for her are growing faster than I thought possible.

As soon as we get back to my house, I crash my lips onto Ainsley's and lift her body, her legs wrapping around me. I sneak my hands under her sweater, feeling her soft skin against my rough one, and make my way up to my bedroom. When I place her on the bed, she reaches the bottom of her sweater and removes it, tossing it on the floor. Her breasts fill up her bra, and I groan. I'm wild when it comes to this woman and want to touch and taste everywhere at once.

Ainsley leans back on her elbows and bends her finger, calling me to her. I move over her, one hand on her stomach, the other holding my weight beside her head. I lean down and trace the seam of her lips with my tongue before she welcomes me into her mouth, her tongue peeking out to mingle with mine. I groan, dropping a bit more weight on her as I move my hips over hers.

"Jeans, off," she pants.

I give her one more deep kiss and move off of her, standing before her as I slowly remove my jeans. She watches with rapt attention as they drop to the floor, followed by my boxer briefs. She toes off her boots while I take off my shirt.

Before I'm back on her, I slide her jeans and underwear down her body, sinking to my knees and pulling her to the edge of the bed.

Her hips buck off the mattress, and a primal cry moves through her as my tongue swipes along her clit.

When my lips suck her into my mouth, her hands fall on my head, tangling in my hair and tugging at the roots.

"Holy shit…" she moans, and I look up at her to see her body squirming, her head pushed back into the bed. I enter a finger into her pussy, continuing to eat her out, pushing her to her climax.

"Knox," she cries out.

"I won't stop until you're satisfied and the only thing falling from those pretty lips of yours is my name on repeat," I say against her, causing her to shiver.

Grinning, I keep my promise until her body grows limp, and her hands loosen their grip on my hair.

"Fuck," she whispers and I chuckle, kissing my way up her body. I lean over her and reach for a condom on my nightstand, rolling it over my cock before pulling her legs apart and settling between her. I kiss her lazily as I align my body with hers and thrust into her.

Her back arches and she meets me, keeping up with my pace, as I get lost in her body and the feel of her walls tightening around my dick.

She's my own heaven. My entire world in one person. And I never thought I'd find this again. Nothing else is better than being with this woman.

As soon as she orgasms again, I let myself go, releasing into her with a grunt and final thrust. I drop my forehead to hers and kiss her nose.

"You're definitely coming to Nashville with me."

Her laughter fills my room, infusing it with happiness that's been missing from this place for a long time.

chapter 18

"Whoa." My arms flail around me, and I almost poke a laughing Knox with the pole in my hand. I glare at him as I find my footing. Skiing is *not* my thing. It all sounded magical when he told me wanted to bring me back to Oaks Resort. That is until I slid my feet into the skis of death and tried to move. Snow meet face. Not my classiest moment.

"Okay." Knox moves as close to me as possible. "Slowly, lean your body forward and use the poles to slide up and keep steady." He demonstrates what he just explained, making it look so easy.

"I'm not born to ski," I complain, following his instructions.

"There you go," he smirks. "You're getting better."

"You're praising me as if I were a six-year-old." I roll my eyes.

"Have I told you I love it when you're all riled up?" He winks in my direction, and part of me wants to kill him, and another part of me wants to throw him on the snow and kiss him silly.

"Okay," I huff and try again, getting the hang of this motion.

"Better." Knox keeps my pace.

"There's no way I can actually ski down a slope," I shake my head, blowing air from the side of my mouth as I concentrate on every single movement.

"We'll see."

"You're insane. I'll sit on that gorgeous porch," I point behind me with the pole, "and watch you ski as I drink something warm."

"You're pretty," he smiles.

"Don't try to sweet talk me now, after you've convinced me to get these death slabs on my feet."

Knox laughs, the sound light and free, and I stop moving to look at him. My goodness, this man has a grip on my heart. When his eyes catch mine, the corners wrinkle with his smile. We're paused in time, eyes staring and heart racing. I'm falling for him.

"How about this?" he breaks up the moment, clearing his throat. "We'll ski for a bit, and then I'll buy you hot chocolate with marshmallows."

"Can it be whipped cream instead?" I tilt my head.

"Whatever you want." He leans in and kisses me. My lips find his in a closed-mouth kiss.

"Crap." I fall back, ass in snow, feet in the air, death slabs barely missing Knox.

Knox's laugh echoes in the open space before he reaches his hand to help me. "Are you okay?"

I glare at him, remaining silent.

"Ainsley?" His eyes widen. "Are you hurt?" I grab hold of his hand and pull him down, risking a ski stabbing me.

"What the…" He lands on the snow, and I guffaw as I watch him struggle to sit up. "You little…" He smashes snow on my face.

"Hey!" I grab a handful and try to spread it on his face, but he's too quick, shifting away from me as my hand slams the ground.

His laughter grows, and I see him lying face up in the snow. I peer up at him with pinched eyebrows.

"You're insane." He wraps his arms around my waist and pulls the top half of my body onto his, kissing me.

"Wouldn't be the first time I hear that," I wink.

Knox sighs contentedly and holds me, pushing his face into the crook of my neck. His breath is warm, and I shiver at the contrast.

"Are you cold?" He drops back his head to look at me.

"A little, but I shivered for another reason," I admit, pressing my lips to his. He groans and brings me closer to him, stupid skis not allowing me to get fully on top of him, which is probably a good thing considering we're in public.

"Let's get that hot chocolate. The sooner we do, the sooner we get back to my place," his voice grows husky.

"I just want to spend time with you," I say.

"Me, too. I look forward to every Wednesday, knowing I have you all to myself."

"Well, that you do." I push my body up to sit. Knox mimics me, sitting before he stands. When he reaches his hand to help me this time, I take hold and pull myself up.

"Come on." He wraps an arm around my neck, and pulls me to him, kissing my temple.

We make our way back to the resort, very slowly, and return the skis. Once I'm off that contraption, I hop up and down and walk around, feeling free to move however I like.

"Happy?" Knox's eyebrows lift up to his forehead, lines creasing there.

"Very." I lean into his side.

"I'm glad." His arm loops around my waist, and we make our way to the café for hot chocolate.

♪

"I know I didn't really ski, but I'm so tired." I wiggle my body on Knox's couch until I'm curled in a ball, holding my glass of wine in one hand.

"Well, that's a shame because I had plans that required more energy than you currently have," he teases.

"Hmm…" I open one eye to look at him sitting next to me with a roguish smile.

"Tease," I lazily drop my free hand on his lap, and he grabs it, linking our fingers.

He kisses my knuckles. "I am teasing you, but I'm happy with what we're doing. Although…" He looks away with uncertainty.

"What?" I perk up, analyzing him.

"I did want to show you something." His smile is shy now, and my curiosity is piqued to what it could be. "It's nowhere near being done," he explains as he stands and grabs his guitar.

My eyes light up, and I move to sit up so I can see him. Sipping my wine, I settle in to hear him sing. "Don't worry about that, I'm excited to hear it."

Knox sits on the accent chair across from the sofa, guitar placed on his lap as his hands position themselves over the neck and strings.

He looks up at me a second before looking back down at the guitar. The music begins to fill the living room, and his deep voice sings.

Dark streets swallowing me in
As I walked blind,
I didn't know which way to go
Or who to trust,
But then I met you

Your touch warmed my skin
And sparked my life,
Your smile shone on me
Another way to live

He finishes off, looking up at me. "It's just the beginning." His leans the guitar against the armrest on the chair.

I place my glass on the coffee table and walk in his direction. Sitting on his lap, his hands immediately move around me. "It's beautiful." I ghost my lips against his. "I can't believe you worked on a song." Hearing him sing, his voice raw without editing or other instruments competing for attention, makes it even more special. The depth and natural talent he owns becomes evident when he sings this way.

"I've got some pretty good inspiration," he smirks.

"Is that so?" I lean back a bit, his hand resting on the curve of my butt.

Knox nods, his expression growing serious. "I wasn't looking to meet anyone. Hell, I wasn't ready, but this, you and me, are proof that we can't control life. I was wrong thinking I wasn't ready, I just hadn't found the right woman."

"Knox," I whisper, tilting my head, my eyes watering. I've never had anyone write a song or poem or anything about me.

His hand comes to the back of my head, pulling my face to his. When he kisses me, I don't wait for him to probe my lips open. I invite him in, tongues dancing to this new beat we're creating. I grip his sweater over his chest and moan, deepening the kiss. His hand on my behind squeezes with desire, and I push my chest flush against his.

I could kiss him for hours.

Knox groans when my phone rings. "Crap. Sorry," I whisper into his mouth.

"'Ts okay," he murmurs, biting my lower lip.

"Mmm…" I breathe out.

"Answer it." He taps my butt when the phone starts ringing again.

I groan, not the good kind, and stand from his lap to fish my phone from my purse. "Hello?" I answer when I see my mom's calling.

"Hi, darlin'," she drawls.

"Hi, Mom. How are you?" I turn to look at Knox, who sits straighter. I bite down my giggle and shake my head.

"I'm good. We're good. I do, however, have some bad news." Her voice is laced with concern.

"What's going on?" I pace around the living room.

"Nothing bad, promise, but we won't be able to make it for Christmas. I'm so sorry, sweetie. I know you were looking forward to us seeing Everton and your apartment. We're in Virginia, snowed in, and they forecast that it will continue for a few more days, here and across the neighboring states."

"It's okay, Mom. I'm glad you guys are safe. Are you staying somewhere where you can get heat and stock up the camper with food?" I stop pacing and listen to her response. I sigh when she assures me they're safe and considering booking a hotel room to wait out the storm.

"I wanted to meet this young man you're dating." My mom attempts to be subtle in bringing up Knox's presence in my life.

"You'll meet him when you can," I turn to look at Knox.

"I looked him up…" her voice trails off, and I grumble, staring up at the ceiling with my eyes closed.

"Mom, you can't believe everything they say." I notice Knox tense and run a hand through his hair. "These last couple of years haven't been easy for him, but trust me when I say he's a good man." I hold Knox's stare.

"I hope so," she exhales, probably worried after what I went through with Bennett.

"You know I'm *usually* a good judge of character," I defend, pacing once again.

"I know, sweetheart. We just want you to be happy," she sighs, and I hear my dad mumbling something in the background.

"Happier than I've ever been," I response and Knox's face relaxes, his brown eyes crinkling in the corners.

"You do sound happy. Hold on."

I furrow my brows, wondering what the hell is going on. "Sweetie?" I hear my dad say.

"Hey, Daddy. I heard you guys are snowed in."

"Yes, I'm sorry we won't make it."

"It's okay. Like I told Mom, I'm just glad you guys are safe. I'll see you when you can make it this way." They don't need to worry or feel guilty.

"Are you sure you're okay? If he hurts you, I'll have to bring out my gun collection," he warns, and I laugh.

I hold my stomach, tossing my head back. "Relax. No need for guns." At that, Knox jumps up from the chair, eyebrows reaching his hairline and his hand gripping the back of his neck.

"Great, now he's scared after hearing me say that," I rein in my laughter.

"Ainsley!" Knox calls out with wide eyes, pacing faster than I was.

"He's there now?" my dad asks.

"Yeah," I shrug as if he could see me.

"Okay, well, we'll talk to you soon. Stay safe and call us if you need anything. We'll keep you updated the more we know about this weather." My dad goes to hang up.

"Dad," I call out. "Thank you. Love you guys."

"Love you, too." I smile and hang up, looking up to see worry lines on Knox's forehead.

"They're dying to meet you," I tease.

"Crap." He tugs his hair, practically pulling it out.

"Stop that." I swat his hands away from his hair and loop my arms around his neck, leaning into him.

"They're just more protective after what happened with my ex-boyfriend. You're a great guy, and they know the media turns things into what they aren't." I play with his hair.

"I don't know. I don't want to mess with a Texan, who has a gun collection." His eyes bug out.

"Relax, it's only about ten guns," I tease.

"Ainsley," Knox growls. "Are you upset they won't make it for Christmas? I know you were counting down the days you had left to see them."

I shrug. "I wish they were coming, but I understand, and rather they stay safe than drive this way in crappy weather and risk something bad happening." My parents and I are close, and the thought of them racing to see me and getting into an accident on the road terrifies me.

"That's true. They'll make it as soon as they can." Knox tries to make me feel better, and I appreciate it.

"They will." I'm sure of it. "Besides, they really do want to meet you." I wink at him and smile. "Now, how about I help you write more of that song."

"You know how to write music?" His eyebrow raises in surprise.

"Nope, but I'm a quick learner. *And* if we get stuck, I can help in different ways," I sway my hips.

His hands run up and down my body before stilling my movements, and he peers down into my eyes. "If we weren't interrupted, I'd already be fucking you. However, I do like the sound of you helping me. We'll call it musician's foreplay," he winks.

"Oh." My eyes pop open, and I bite down on my lips. Knox chuckles and slaps my ass. I join him on the couch, guitar in his hand, and get prepared to learn how to write a song.

chapter 19

Knox

When I left Nashville, I could've sworn I'd retire my guitar and put music behind me. I'm not so sure at the moment. It was therapeutic to work on this song, though it took me longer than usual. I felt the way I did at the beginning of my career. If I pick this up again, it will definitely have to be on my terms, so I can feel that passion run through me and put out music I'm proud of.

For the past hour, Ainsley and I have been tossing ideas for the song. She's thrown ideas my way, inspiring me, but nothing has quite worked into the current song.

"What about this?" she asks, tapping her chin. "You've made it easy, sweeping me away, and making me believe in more than heartache." Her round eyes wait for my reaction.

"I like that," I nod. It could be a bridge in the song, leading into the second part.

"Really?" She bounces on the cushions and clasps her hands together. I've never written a song with a girlfriend, but something about doing this with her, as if she's helping me find my place again, feels right.

"Yeah." I write it down on the paper I grabbed earlier to test it all out when we're done.

"Let's hear it," she asks, pushing her hair behind her ear.

Okay, I guess I'm testing it now. Her proud smile affects me, wanting to give her whatever she wants. I begin strumming the chords, the music still imperfect as we get this just right. As I start singing, she looks at me as if I'm a hero, giving me devotion I don't deserve. She's the one who's given me hope—I should be worshipping her.

Dark streets swallowing me in
As I walked blind,
I didn't know which way to go
Or who to trust,
But then I met you

Your touch warmed my skin
And sparked my life,
Your smile shone on me
Another way to live

You've made it easy,
sweeping me away
and making me believe
in more than heartache

You make it easy to love
When I promised I'd never
Open up to another

I add the last verse without thinking. Ainsley reaches out and places her hand on my thigh. "I think that's a great addition," she praises, her hand comforting. She's so patient and understanding, and she doesn't judge my past or my actions.

"Thanks," I keep my voice quiet.

"What got you into music?" she asks, leaning back and gazing at my guitar.

I grin. "My grandfather was a musician. Not famous, but he played locally. The people here loved hearing and watching him perform. Being the older grandchild, I spent a lot of time with him around the ranch growing up, and he taught me to play. After, I started taking classes and learning songwriting."

"Do you know how to play any other instruments?"

I nod, "The piano."

"Really?" Her excitement makes me chuckle. "I can't play any instrument for the life of me, and you've already heard me sing." Her eyebrows rise and a shy smirk lifts the corners of her lips.

"You can sing to me any time." I drop the guitar next to me on the couch and pull her to me. "I like hearing you sing, off-pitch and all," I wink, holding back my laugh as I tease her.

"Please," she rolls her eyes and pushes my chest.

"I do because you don't hide from me," I kiss her lips.

"I wouldn't do that," her voice grows serious.

"You have no idea how much I appreciate that." I hold her face, her hair covering part of it. She reaches up and combs it away, moving it to the side so I can get a full view of her beautiful face. "Sexy." I waggle my eyebrows.

Ainsley laughs and squeezes my cheeks with a hand, forcing my lips to pucker. She gives them a peck before saying, "You're sexy."

"I plan to show you just how sexy I can be." I move my lips down her jaw to her neck, sucking her earlobe between my teeth and scraping them gently. When she moans, I carry her and place her on top of me as she straddles my lap.

"Oh, you can definitely show me that," she says on a whimper, grinding into my erection.

Standing, I hold her ass firmly and walk us up to my bedroom. All the laughter and teasing is gone as I drop her on the bed and strip her naked, ready to make the world disappear and hear her call out my name on repeat like my favorite song.

♪

I groan as my phone wakes me up. Who the hell is calling me this early? I turn in my bed, my eyes still closed, and feel Ainsley wiggle closer to me. I drop an arm around her and pull her closer to me. She lets out a soft sigh in her sleep, and I crack my eyes open to look at her. Mussed hair and parted lips meet my gaze, and I smile. She's peace and happiness, and I want her in my life permanently.

My hand finds her bare ass, and I pull her toward me until one of her legs drapes over mine. My morning wood hardens even more, feeling her heat. I squeeze her ass, and she moans. I wonder if she's really asleep or pretending so she doesn't have to get up just yet.

I move my head to kiss her lips, and she mumbles, "Sleep."

I chuckle and then sigh when my phone starts ringing again.

"Answer it," she protests and turns over, balling her body into the fetal position.

I shake my head and grin, getting out of bed to answer my damn phone. Seeing the name on the screen, I growl, "This better be important."

"You didn't tell me you were seeing someone," Harris says, exasperated.

"My relationship status isn't your business." Annoyance ringing loud and clear.

"It is when the media gets a hold of the news and starts printing it everywhere." I freeze.

"What?"

"You two looked very cozy at a resort, romantic and all, but you're front page news on a few sites and entertainment magazines."

"Shit." I run a hand through my hair and turn to look at Ainsley sleeping on my bed.

"People are curious. Your divorce just became final, and remember the public doesn't know about the truth of your marriage, so for them, this is a surprise," he explains what I already know.

"Yeah, yeah. How bad is it?" I blow out air and throw on a pair of sweats before I sneak out of the room, so I don't wake Ainsley up.

"Well, you've got the cheating bastard article, the other woman who tore your marriage apart one, and the third best would have to do."

I shut my eyes and pinch the bridge of my nose. "You're kidding me?"

"You know how this works," he says flatly.

"I'll release a statement," I say as if that will fix everything.

"I think you should lay low, keep this to yourself until things blow over. Give people a chance to process the divorce before being public with another woman," Harris suggests.

"No." It's a definite response. "Been down that road, and I'm not gonna do that again. I care about her." I walk down to the kitchen and turn on the coffee maker. "I'm not keeping her in the dark."

"Knox, it's only going to get worse before it gets better. This is just the beginning. When they find out her name and where she works, they'll be going after her, asking questions, chasing her down."

I take a deep breath, begging for patience. "I won't let them."

At this, Harris laughs. "Come on, you can't control that."

As I'm filling a mug with coffee, Ainsley walks into the kitchen wearing one of my sweatshirts that stops mid-thigh, her legs taunting me. *Fuck me.* Her eyebrows are pinched together, and her head is tilted, trying to read me.

"Let me think," I tell Harris, staring at her.

"You don't have much time to think. Before you know it, the paps will be in Everton, if they aren't there already." I know he's right. This was only a matter of time, but I was hoping people wouldn't twist this into a scandal. I should've known better.

"I'll call you later." I don't take my eyes away from Ainsley's.

"Bye," he sounds miffed.

I hang up the phone. "Coffee?" I ask.

"Yes," she nods slowly, her eyes narrowed.

I fix her coffee, adding cream, and hand it to her. "Thanks," she says as she sits on one of my stools. "Now, tell me what's going on." Her hands wrap around the mug as she keeps her gaze on me.

I exhale loudly and brace myself on the counter. "Our relationship is out in the open. That was Harris, my manager. Apparently, there are photos of us together at the lodge yesterday. The media has spun every story possible and published it." My hand abuses my hair.

Ainsley is quiet, drinking her coffee. When she places the mug on the counter, she reaches her hand out.

"What?" I raise my eyebrows.

"Give me your phone, please." I close my eyes and hand her the device. She begins typing, her eyes scanning the screen. I haven't seen any of the articles, so I wait for her assessment, shoulders tense.

"Huh." She keeps reading, and I'm barely able to hold onto the bit of patience I have. Her eyes lift to mine. "This isn't good." Her lips pinch together as she turns the phone for me to read the screen.

I skim the article, nostrils flaring. *Knox Bentley has moved on already. Not only did he ruin his marriage with Amelia Stanford by cheating on her with Reese Stone, but now he's cozying up with a blonde that gives us serious Amelia vibes. Maybe he regrets his divorce and is using this mystery woman as an Amelia placeholder. We can conclude that this woman is the cause for our favorite music couple to head to Splitsville. What do you think about Knox's mystery woman?*

"This is bullshit," I growl. At the same time, my Google alert pops up in my notifications. I click on the link and read. "Fuck," I scream.

"What?" She sits taller, leaning forward with wide eyes.

"They found out who you are and published your name. I'm so sorry, Ainsley." I walk around the counter and hold her hands. "I didn't think this would be so bad." I shake my head.

"Hey." She reaches up to touch my face. "This isn't your fault. We knew it was bound to happen. Sure, we didn't expect so much made-up crap, but people are assholes and drama sells."

"I hate it," I say through my clenched teeth.

"It's not fun, that's for sure. What do you want to do?" She tilts my head down so she can look into my eyes. "This is your image."

I shake my head. "It's ours. Yours is just as important as mine. You may not be famous, *yet,* but you also have an image and are just as important as I am in all of this. I don't want this to ruin your life."

197

"Knox, being with you will never ruin my life." Her words are soft, gentle. "I don't want you to have to go through more hurt than you already have. It's not fair to you that people are dicks."

I chuckle dryly. "I don't deserve you," I shake my head.

"Hey," her brows come together, and she frowns. "That's not true. You deserve to be happy, and I'm just lucky that I make you happy," she winks.

"You're incredible." I cup the side of her face, and she leans into it, sighing.

"If you want to take some time apart, at least in public, I'll be okay with that."

"No," I shoot out before she can finish that sentence. "That's not an option. People will always talk, whether they see us together today or three months from now." I'm adamant about this.

"What do you want to do then?" she asks.

"It won't be easy, and I know I have no right to ask you for patience and strength, but I want people to know you're a part of my life. If you're okay with that, of course. I've already kept one relationship hidden in the past, and I refuse to lose you over this. Not you." My teeth grind together. She means too much to me. I knew I couldn't hide here forever, pretending people would magically forget who I am. I'm older and wiser this time around, and I'm not backing down from a fight. I just hope she's willing to stand beside me.

"Of course, I want to be with you. I know we haven't been together for too long, but I'm willing to push

through this. So, they called me a homewreckin' whore?"
she shrugs. "I want to say I've been called worse, but I
actually haven't," there's a hint of humor in her voice,
and I start to loosen up.

"I'm sorry." I lean my forehead on hers.

"Stop apologizing." I open my eyes.

"If anyone asks you questions, ignore them. You
keep walking as if no one were there, got it?" I have to
make sure she's safe, but I won't be with her twenty-four
hours a day, seven days a week. "These people are
ruthless," I warn.

"Okay." She nods quickly.

"I'll do everything I can to smooth this over," I
assure her.

"We got this." Her smile is small, nervous, but I
appreciate her attitude.

"Okay then," I squeeze her thigh, praying everything
turns out okay. "Breakfast?" I ask.

"I guess it wouldn't be smart to go out and eat
somewhere?" Her eyes open wide.

"Probably not," I respond, feeling as if now she's
going to have to measure each step in her life because of
me, restrict herself from the things she loves.

"Darn. I was craving those stuffed, French toasts
from Beehive." She licks her lips, causing me to laugh.

"What if I call and see if they'll deliver?" I'll pay triple
the price if I need to.

"Really?" she perks up.

"Anything for you." I kiss her softly. "I just wish I
hadn't received this news when you were dressed like

that. This morning did not go as I planned." I let my words linger between us, full of meaning.

"Knox, we can't control everything. We need to learn to navigate life as it comes our way," she shares her words of wisdom.

"You're right. I just wish I could protect you from this," I tell her.

"I knew the consequences of dating you, and I made a choice after having weighed my options."

"I wish I would've done the same. Had I known they'd make you out to be the bad guy, I would've kept my distance." The words are out before I can process them, and her face drops with a frown.

"Really?" She looks up at me with sad eyes, and I feel like the world's largest prick.

"Fuck. That didn't come out the right way. I just… I don't want you to have to go through this. I don't want people to automatically think wrongly about you when you're an amazing person," I try to mend what I said, but the damage is done. Her entire body shifts, more closed off, her energy pushing me away.

"Fuck," I mumble on a breath and grab my phone. "Breakfast?" I ask.

She nods in silence, taking a drink from her mug and shivering. Ainsley walks to the microwave and warms up her coffee, arms hugging her body. She looks out the big windows onto the patio, staring at the white ground.

I shut my eyes closed and dial Beehive's number, hoping to God they'll deliver that French toast.

chapter 20

Ainsley

I haven't been at work for more than twenty minutes, and I already want to sprint out the back door and go home. As soon as I walked in, the few people who were sitting at the bar stared with curiosity. I'm sure it's entertaining that the new girl in town fished the local celebrity, considering not much else happens around here.

After breakfast, I got dressed and left Knox's house with the excuse I had to go grocery shopping before work. He didn't buy my lie, but he took me home anyway. Hearing him say he would've stayed away from me had he known how bad things could get was painful, even if I knew what he meant to say. Knowing he would have fought his feelings for me when I couldn't do that, made me feel insecure.

Knox is a great man, and I have no doubt that he cares about me. I know that. I repeat this to myself as I work and ignore questions as he advised.

I serve drinks and quickly move onto another task to not engage in conversations that can be misunderstood or manipulated into something else. People around here had already seen us together for a few weeks, so I don't know why the sudden interest. I guess people do love the drama, and now we're no longer Ainsley and Knox, Everton residents. Now, we're Knox, the famous musician, and Ainsley, the other woman.

Gah, I can't believe people buy into that crap.

I hold in my scream and throw on a fake smile. "Hi." I look at the woman leaning over the bar. "Can I get a beer?"

"Sure." I grab her usual drink and pop the cap before pouring it in a glass.

"Thanks." She hands me a ten. "So… I didn't know you and Knox were dating. That's cool," she smiles so sweetly, I fear I'll get cavities from staring at her.

I nod, my mouth in a flat line. I wasn't good enough to be her friend when I was just Ainsley, new girl in town and bartender. Now, she's suddenly interested in making small-talk. Thanks, but I'll pass.

I turn around to do anything that will make me not have to talk to her, but she stays in her spot. "I've known him my entire life. He and Axel," she keeps talking, and I roll my eyes, my back to her. "Anyway, I think it's really cool." I want to tell her she already said it was cool, but bite my tongue. "Maybe one day we can all hang out."

Ah, there it is.

I turn to face her. "Maybe." If I weren't at work, I'd say something less nice. Actually, I probably wouldn't, I'd just ignore her. I don't want fake friends.

"Hey." Knox arrives and takes a seat, looking between the other woman and me. I knew he wouldn't take long to show up.

"Hi, Knox," she smiles, way too excited. I lift my eyebrows, and she reels in her happiness.

"Hey, Emma. How you doing?" He takes a seat, smiling at me.

"Great, I was just telling Ainsley we should all hang out sometime," Emma keeps talking.

"Oh, now you care to be friends with her?" Knox doesn't hold back, and I bite down my lips and widen my eyes at him.

"What?" Emma looks between us, holding her breath.

"Ainsley's been living here for months, and you never tried to get to know her, but now that's she's dating me you suddenly care. We're good," he dismisses her, and she stumbles back, knocked into silence.

I look at Knox, my eyes popping out of my head. "Knox," I say quietly, locking my jaw.

"Don't look at me that way. I won't let someone try to use you or think I'm an idiot."

I sigh and shake my head, filling a glass of scotch for him.

"Thank you." His fingers graze mine, and I relax.

"You're welcome," I breathe out softly, still hurt.

"I'm sorry about what I said earlier," he whispers, his eyes cast down. When they look back at me, I see pain etched on them.

"We'll talk later," I nod, scratching my forehead.

"So, you two *are* shacking up?" I look up to see Eli standing next to Knox.

I groan, and Knox curses. "Watch it," he warns him.

"Whoa," Eli raises his hands in surrender and laughs, taking a seat next to him. "I mean, I did notice the flirting, but I didn't know it was official."

"Beer?" I ask him.

"Please," he winks, and Knox glares at him.

"Ah, you're cute when you're jealous," he teases Knox, and I giggle.

As the hours pass, more people ask questions, unashamed of the invasion of privacy as if they deserve a glance into our personal lives, and whisper amongst themselves as they point at Knox and me. At least be subtle if you're going to gossip about someone who is standing in front of you. Every person who asks me a question I don't want to answer makes me feel more uncomfortable. I don't want the locals here to see me differently.

"Hey, Bentley, you couldn't be happy with your city girls, you had to go and fuck one of ours," Mr. McFord yells across the bar. I freeze, the glass I'm holding almost falling to the floor. I look at Knox, my eyes growing. He jumps off the stool and stalks toward Mr. McFord.

"Knox," I call out and shake my head. He barely looks at me before he grabs Mr. McFord by the collar and lifts him.

"What the fuck did you say?" I've never seen him this angry.

"Ya heard me, kid." I'm impressed the old man doesn't flinch despite Knox towering over him.

"Back off, McFord." His warning is so calm, it causes me to shiver. Still frozen, I watch and wait, trying to telecommunicate with Knox. The last thing he needs is a fight on record.

"Knox, patience," I say, hoping he takes his own advice. His eyes meet mine, and I tilt my head, smiling softly. I sigh when he releases Mr. McFord and begins walking back to his seat.

The entire bar is silent, witnessing this interaction.

Mr. McFord laughs boastfully, his big belly shaking. "Pussy-whipped."

Before I know what's happening, a scream leaves my mouth as Knox turns and punches McFord in the jaw. The older man stumbles back, gripping his face and glaring at Knox. Eli is by his side immediately, holding him back.

"Respect her," he growls.

Knox's body trembles with anger, and he shakes off his hand. I'm around and by his side in a second. I stand before him and grab his face. "Stop." I stare into his eyes, pleading with him.

His jaw is slack, and his nostrils are flared. I get on my toes and kiss him, hoping to break his anger spell. "Please," I whisper against his lips.

It's as if he finally sees me, his hands going to my waist and pulling me into a hug. He sneaks his face into the crook of my neck, inhaling deep and slow.

"It's okay," I whisper.

"It's not. Are you okay?" He lifts his head, his eyes scanning my face.

"Yeah. Are you?" I grab his right hand and stare at his knuckles.

"I will be," he mumbles, lifting a brow as he stares over my shoulder.

"Come on." I drag him by the hand and make him sit on the stool again. I walk around the bar and look around at everyone. Some faces are scared, others are curious.

"Show's over, folks," I call out, rolling my eyes.

"I want a man that stands up for me that way," someone sighs in the crowd.

Knox is staring at his trembling hands, resting on top of the bar, silent. Eli looks up at me and shakes his head, unsure of what to do or say. I take a few deep breaths to slow my racing heart and get back to tending the customers ordering another round.

I sneak glances at Knox while working, his position the same—staring at his hands and his body stiff. I stand in front of him when I finish serving the drink I'm preparing. "Drink." I push the scotch closer to him.

His hand reaches out to mine quickly. "I'm sorry," he whispers, his eyes lifting to mine.

"Thank you for defending me," I tell him. "Now, have a drink, and we'll talk later. I'm not mad, though," I assure him.

I've never had a shift drag on like it did tonight. Wishing it were time to go home, I stay as busy as possible and ignore anyone who isn't placing a drink order. By the time my shift ends, I want to race out of the building and call in sick tomorrow. I've never been one to let people's opinions get to me, but this is on a whole other level.

"Ready?" Knox meets me by the door.

"Yeah." I nod.

"I'll follow you home unless you want to come home with me." He's still sullen, probably feeling guilty if I know him.

"It's okay. It's been an emotional and heavy day. I'm going to go home, and we'll talk tomorrow."

"Ainsley," he shifts his head and raises a brow. "No."

"Knox. I'm tired. It's been a crazy day, and I just want to sleep. This has nothing to do with us, I promise." I hold his hand and let him walk me to my car.

"I'll call you in the morning. I'll grab some coffees and bagels and take them to your house when I wake up," I suggest, needing a few hours to decompress.

"I guess I don't have a choice," he crosses his arms.

I hug his middle, resting my head on his arms until he sighs and hugs me back. "We're okay," I make sure he knows I'm not upset at him. This situation simply sucks.

"I rather follow you home, but call me if you need me. Okay?" He looks at me, lifting my chin, so I'm staring into his eyes.

"Promise." His lips touch mine briefly before I climb into my car. For some reason, things feel dense between us, as if any second the weight of this will crack us.

I drive home, careful of the snow and focusing on my breath to clear my mind. After a good night's sleep, I'll feel better and be able to tackle this with optimism. I hope.

When I pull into the parking lot of my apartment building, I see a crowd standing by the entrance. I squint my eyes toward them, wondering what the hell is going on. When someone looks my way, noticing my running car, I see a flash. I cover my eyes with my hands as I hear commotion a few steps away.

"Fuck," I yell in my car and slam the steering wheel before grabbing my phone and calling Knox, heart racing. I see people running toward my car, and I throw the car in reverse, pulling out of my spot while hitting 'Speaker' on my screen and praying Knox answers right away.

"Hello?"

"Knox," my voice shakes.

"What's wrong?" He sounds worried when he hears me speak.

"The paparazzi found where I live. There's a huge crowd outside my building. When they saw my car, they snapped photos, but I pulled out before they could reach my car."

"Fuck, I'm on my way. I should've followed you home," he yells in frustration.

"Meet me at Clarke's, and I'll leave my car there. I don't want to drive to your place, they'll just follow me.

"Fine. Ainsley?" he pauses.

"Yeah?"

"Drive safely, please," his worry deepens as he pleads.

"I promise."

I make it back to the bar as quickly as I can, checking the rearview mirror in case anyone is following me, and exhale when the road is dark behind me.

I pull into Clarke's parking and see Knox's headlights waiting for me. I rush to his car and jump in, barely closing the door before he's speeding home.

We're both quiet on the drive over. Knox continues to torment his hair with his hand, which is now a mess of wild waves. By the time we make it to his house, I'm deflated and exhausted. Maybe I should've pushed through the photographers and gone home.

I follow Knox into his house, thankful he has a garage we can hide in, the silence making my skin crawl. He drops on the couch, his expression stone. I stand, unsure of my place.

"Today has been hell," he finally speaks.

"Tell me about it." I look at him from the entrance of the living room.

His arms lift, reaching out to me, so I go to him. He pulls me onto his lap. "I'm sorry. You don't deserve my crappy attitude and anger. I screwed up earlier, and I haven't let that go. Then, Old McFord talks shit, and the paparazzi find your apartment, and it's all a fuckin' mess. I moved here to avoid all of this." His head drops back on the couch, his pained expression tearing my heart apart.

"Hey." I wait for him to look at me. "I admit that it hurt to hear you say that you wouldn't have pursued me had you known this would happen. I wish I can be someone worth fighting for," I look away.

"Ainsley, you are. Don't you see that? What I said, it came out all wrong." He shakes his head. "What I meant was that I didn't want to put you in this position where you're now getting hauled by people. Trust me, I wouldn't be able to stay away from you. You've captivated me. Hell, I started writing music because of you. You inspire me, and that's something I'll never regret.

"You're the only woman I want in my life, and someone worth every single fight. Harris suggested keeping our relationship hidden for a while, same as you did, and I told him that wasn't an option. I'm proud to have you by my side." He cups my face, his thumbs moving back and forth across my cheeks. "You're the woman I want in my life, day in and day out," he repeats. "I'll fight whoever I need to in order to keep you safe and by my side. I'm sorry I fucked up."

I nod. "I guess I took it to heart. I should know how you feel about me without you having to say it, but I also compare myself to the other women you've had in your life—"

He interrupts me. "They don't compare to you. You're funny, genuine, beautiful, and have a heart of gold. Don't compare yourself, because you're cutting yourself short with the way I see you." He tilts my head down and kisses my forehead. "Promise you believe me."

"I do, but that doesn't change the fact that your life could be easier without me in it."

"No." He shakes his head fiercely. "If it's not you, it'll be something else they spin. Believe me."

"So what do we do?" I ask.

"Let me think, but for now, you'll stay here. We'll grab some clothes and whatever else you need tomorrow." He slowly starts to relax, and I place my head on his shoulder. Knox holds me as my eyes grow heavy, keeping me safe despite his guilt swallowing him up.

chapter 21

Knox

These last few days have been hell. Between the photographers spread out in this town and my relationship with Ainsley in turmoil, I want to send everyone to hell and sneak away with her. To make matters worse, we're at my parents' house for Christmas Eve dinner, and they keep asking us how we're doing. I'm glad it's only us five tonight and not my extended family adding to the interrogation.

Ainsley pretends she's okay with it all, but I notice her faraway look when she thinks she's alone.

I hate that it's because of me that she's experiencing this. The only upside is that the locals have calmed down. I'm sure watching me hit McFord put things into perspective. I won't let anyone hurt Ainsley. As for me, the media caught wind of my "bar fight" and added to the story, saying I have a dangerous jealous streak and Ainsley's with me for fear that I'll hit her. The ridiculousness of it all almost makes me laugh. Almost. If it weren't my life they're ruining.

"Are you ready for your performance on New Year's Eve?" my mom asks.

"Yeah."

"Are you going with him?" She looks at Ainsley.

"Um…" Her round eyes sweep up to me. "I'm not sure yet."

"Yes, she is," I answer my mom and raise my eyebrows at Ainsley.

"I need to make sure work will give me the night and the next day off. It's a busy time," she explains, but I know she's stalling. She was going to ask Adam for the days off a week ago.

"I hope they do. It's amazing to watch him perform live," my mom adds as if I weren't sitting at the table with them. It's clear she senses the tension between us. Anyone within a fifty-mile radius of us could feel the tension.

With all of this, my probability of going back to a music career is diminishing. It's a reminder of why I decided to take a step back.

"Who's ready for dessert?" My mom continues to bring some normalcy to our dinner.

"Me," my dad smiles at her.

"I'll help you clean up," Ainsley offers, grabbing my empty plate with hers. I smile up at her, desperate to fix this.

"Thank you." My mom takes her up on her offer.

"Dude, what the hell?" Axel blows out air and grips the back of his neck.

I shake my head, rubbing my eyes.

I feel my dad clasp my shoulder, and I turn my head to him. "Every couple goes through some hardships. It's whether or not you're willing to fight for each other that will make you or break you." He squeezes my shoulder.

I nod, appreciative of his encouragement, but still feeling like shit.

"She could be living a peaceful life like she was before I showed up, no one harassing her."

"Well, son, if you ask me, I'd tell you that woman in the kitchen with your momma loves you, so I doubt she'd agree with you." My dad nods as if he's certain of his observation.

I raise my eyebrows, and he laughs. "Don't look at me that way. I know when a woman loves a man, and Ainsley is in love with you. Give her time to catch up, she may not know it yet."

I remain silent and look at Axel, who's leaning back in his seat with a cocky smile.

"Okay, we have apple pie and pumpkin pie," my mom interrupts us as she walks back into the dining room with Ainsley following closely behind her.

"I know pumpkin pie is supposed to be a Thanksgiving dessert and all that, but I *love* it and only eat it this time of year, so I made it again. Hope that's okay." I bite down my smile as she rambles on and on, reminding me of that day in the coffee shop.

"We love pumpkin pie, don't we?" My dad looks at the two of us.

"Hell yes." Axel grins.

"Yup, especially yours," I say and reach for her hand under the table once she's back at her seat. I lace our fingers together, keeping some part of her in my hold, needing to feel her. She looks at me with a soft smile, and if I'm not mistaken, water in her eyes. I lift our hands and kiss her knuckles, not caring that we have an audience. Her chest drops with a sigh, and for the first time in a few days, she relaxes.

This has been hard on us both, and I haven't taken the time to really see her, feel her while I've tried to figure out how to deal with the disaster of the media. I vow to make sure she's truly doing okay once we leave here, talk to her, and see what's going on in her mind. We're in this together, and we've been dealing with it separately. If we want our relationship to work, we need to communicate.

"We'll see you tomorrow for lunch and gifts." My mom walks us to the door.

"Thank you for having me again," Ainsley says, hugging my mom.

"Nonsense. There's no way you were going to stay home. Besides, you're part of the family now." My mom gives me a pointed look with a smile. I don't know if to thank her or expect a lecture the next time we're alone.

"Thanks, Mom." I kiss her cheek and guide Ainsley to the car, opening her door.

I hold her hand once I'm in the driver's seat and drive back to my place. I'm silent on the trip back, trying to organize my thoughts so we could talk, and hope to fix this. I miss our easy relationship, and right now, things are complicated. Between photographers stalking both of us, showing up at her apartment and job, and the mean rumors continuing to grow in the entertainment business, we've lost the spark in our relationship.

I park the truck in my driveway, and Ainsley is out of her seat before I can make my way to open her door. I sigh and reach for her hand, gripping it.

"Let's talk," I say as I unlock the front door.

We make our way to the living room, and I sit on the couch next to her. When I turn to face her, I notice unshed tears in her eyes and pull her to me, wrapping my arms around her slender body. Feeling her rapidly beating heart breaks my heart.

"What's going on?" I lean back a bit to look into her eyes, silent trails of tears on her face. My thumb does quick work of drying them.

"I don't know," she whispers, her teeth gnawing her bottom lip.

"I need you to talk to me."

She shakes her head, looking away from me.

"Ainsley, please," I beg, feeling helpless.

"This is so hard," her words come out tangled. "I just… I'm trying to be strong, ignore everyone following me around, the lies they're printing. I want to be with you…" her voice trails.

I lock my jaw, my chest heaving. I refuse to let this career take her away from me. It already stole too much from me, but I won't let her be one of them. I rub my eyes and let my hand slide down my face in exasperation, tugging my beard.

"What do you want?"

She leans back, flinching at my tone. My words come out harsh, but I don't mean to direct my anger at her. "I'm sorry. I'm not mad at you, but I hate that my past is ruining this. I hate that once again, my career choice is taking away what I want most in life."

"I thought by now they'd realize there's no real story and would leave town," she says.

"I was hoping the same thing," I admit. "I'll talk to Harris again and see what we can do. Unfortunately, we can't really press charges if they don't touch us or cause any threats."

"They're invading our lives," her voice rises.

"I know. Trust me, I've lived with this for years." I tear my hair from the roots with the force of my hand.

"I go into work, and a photographer is waiting for me at the bar, Knox."

"What do you want?" I ask her again. "I'll give you whatever you want, even if it means letting you go." I don't want to cause her any more hurt, and seeing the pain in her face is breaking me. I can't protect her like I wish I could. We don't live in a snow-filled bubble, no matter how much it felt that way when we first started dating. As it is, it's only been two months and look at all the damage I've brought into her life.

Ainsley shakes her head. "I don't want that. Do you?" Her eyebrows furrow, her mouth frowning, her eyes filling with tears again.

"Of course not, but I don't know how to keep you away from this."

"You can't," she says with resignation. "Even if we broke up, people will want to know what happened." She deflates, melting into the cushion.

"I just want you to be happy again." I've stolen her joy and replaced it with worry and fear. She silently nods. "We need to talk if we want to overcome this," I add.

"I know. It's Christmas, though. Can we forget about it for tonight?"

I nod, although I disagree. Pretending this isn't real, even for a night, isn't the solution.

"I have your gift," she whispers. "How about I give it to you tonight, seeing it's technically Christmas day."

"Okay." I humor her because she deserves to be put first.

I watch Ainsley stand and walk to the Christmas tree we both decorated, picking up the long box I've been curious about. It's too light and narrow to be a new guitar, I snuck in one afternoon and held it to try to guess what's in it.

"Here." Her smile reappears, and she sits next to me. "I hope you like it."

"I'm sure I will." I tear the gold paper and lift the lid of the box. I run my fingers over the soft leather.

"Wow," I whisper, picking up the guitar strap and smiling genuinely for the first time in days. The strap has the phrase, You're the chili to my Frito pie, engraved on it.

I chuckle, meeting her eyes. "I don't like it, I love it. Thanks, babe," I lean forward to kiss her.

"I'm so glad you do." Her eyes light up, a semblance of the real Ainsley peeking through.

A different sensation fills me as I watch her pride and look back at the gift she got for me, meaningful on so many levels. She's the reason I picked up my guitar again in months, the reason I'm smiling and living. I'm falling in love with her, and I'm afraid I'll lose her.

I stand and grab the small box under the tree, sitting next to her before I place her gift on her lap. "Open it."

She looks up at me from beneath her lashes, a small smile forming on her lips. She rips the Christmas trees printed wrapping, not as gentle as I was, and I have to laugh at her enthusiasm. When her fingers open up the box, she gasps.

"This is beautiful." She stares at the gold snowflake necklace. Her finger runs over the small diamond in the center.

"You're like a snowflake—perfect, full of magic, and unique. That first snowball fight, where you didn't take pity on me or feed into my bullshit, you were simply yourself, that's when I knew you were special. I realized then that although my life was a mess, I wanted to get to know you. I wanted more than run-ins in random places. I wanted to be as brave as you are, and you inspired me to take my life back in my own hands, without knowing you did." I hold her gaze as I speak, confessing the moment I wanted Ainsley in my life.

"I love it." She leaps forward and hugs me. Maybe she was onto something when she asked to exchange gifts tonight. I hold her to me, exhaling the tension. Her lips touch my cheek, and I tighten my arms around her.

"Thank you," she whispers into my ear, my skin shivering. I keep her close to me, breathing in her sweet scent as I pray we can work through this bump before it does more damage than we can repair.

chapter 22

Knox

I pull the heavy door at Clarke's entrance, my body feeling like lead. I blink slowly, pushing my hair back and covering my face when I notice a man pointing his camera at me. Why the hell hasn't Adam kicked these people out yet?

I sit at the bar, looking around for Ainsley. I didn't want her to go home alone before coming into work, but she insisted on grabbing a few more things from her place and assured me she'd be okay.

I couldn't fight her. Christmas was better, but we're still not one-hundred-percent. I feel like any wrong comment will push her further away. I'm tired. Tired of losing my life to my name, my persona.

Not seeing Ainsley, I wave Adam down. "What can I get you?"

"Where's Ainsley?" My eyebrows lift. He looks at me as if I'm crazy, eyebrows bunched together and mouth set in a straight line.

"She didn't tell you?" He throws the rag in his hand over his shoulder and crosses his arms.

"Tell me what?" I demand.

"She was let go."

"What? When?" I slam my hand on the bar.

"About an hour ago." He blows out a deep breath.

"What the fuck?" I growl. "Why?"

"Something about the paparazzi interfering with our place of business." He keeps it brief but makes sure I know her lack of a job is my fault. I shake my head and stand, pushing the stool so far back it almost hits someone. I stalk out of the bar and jump in my truck. If one of these photographers gets in my way, I'm running them over. I'm fucking over them being here.

I go straight to her apartment and bang on her door.

"What?" Her shoulders slump when she opens the door with bloodshot eyes.

"Ainsley," I draw out and hug her. She fights me, pushing my chest back. "Why didn't you call me right away?" It hurts that she came home and didn't reach out to me, knowing I was going to see her.

She shakes her head and turns, walking further into her house. I lock the door and follow her into the living room.

"I didn't want to add more to your plate. I knew you'd take this on and blame yourself," her voice is flat, her body slumped in defeat.

"It is my fault," I grit my teeth.

"No," she shakes her head. "It just sucks because I really liked that job. I guess I couldn't be a bartender my entire life," she says to herself.

I reach for her hand, and she lets me hold it despite her shoulders tensing. "I don't know how to fix this. I've tried talking to them, posting on social media, this is what they live off of. Unfortunately, this brings them joy, and

222

they're selfish to not care about the consequences in our lives."

She swipes her hands over her cheeks, and it kills me to know she's experiencing this because she's in a relationship with me. I can't shake the guilt.

"I'm gonna stay here tonight," she says, her teeth torturing her lips.

"Are you sure?" I tilt my head and squint my eyes.

"Yeah. I think it's for the best. Just a few days, I need to clear my head." I won't lie and say that doesn't hurt, but she has no right to put up with my shit.

"You'll call me?" I stare into her eyes, the red around them clouding the brightness in her baby blues.

"Yeah," she nods.

"And New Year's?" I risk asking.

"I think you should go alone, it's for the best. We don't need to draw more attention to ourselves, and maybe we need a few days apart to think things through."

"I don't need to think anything through when it comes to us. I want you, plain and simple," I fight against her words.

"I need some time," she shakes her head, tears drowning out her words.

"I'm yours, no one else's. They can try to tear us apart, but I'm comin' back to you," I promise.

"I'm sorry," she hiccups.

"Don't apologize, you have no reason to. I know how hard this is, and I've had years to get accustomed to it, yet it still irks me. I'm going to fix this though." I need a real plan, starting by running these people out of town and getting them to stop printing lies.

I lean forward and kiss her softly. When I stand, I reach for her hand. "Lock up behind me."

She nods and stands. At the door, I turn to look at her and hold her for a few seconds, inhaling her flowery scent, memorizing it. "I'll call you," I guarantee.

"Bye, Knox." She says it as if it's a final goodbye, but I won't lose her that easily.

Once I'm in my car, I call Harris.

"Schedule an exclusive interview with Music & Life Magazine," I tell him as soon as I hear the call pick up, not letting him speak.

"Okay." He doesn't question my motives.

"And book a private plane to and from Nashville. I'll be in and out as soon as I finish my song." I don't wait for him to speak. I hang up, slam my steering wheel, and speed home.

♪

Ainsley: good luck tomorrow

Knox: thanks… I'll miss you

Ainsley: you'll do great. i'll see you when you get back

Knox: yeah…

Knox: did u see the latest?

Ainsley: ugh yes.

Knox: i'm fixin it

Ainsley: thanks

Knox: are you okay?

Ainsley: yup

I squeeze my eyes shut and grip the back of my neck. She's not okay. I put my phone back down and finish packing the few things I need for Nashville tomorrow. Ainsley and I have barely spoken since I left her house three days ago. Our text conversations are about as intimate as the one we just had, and our phone calls are few and far between—all of them short and superficial. We may not have broken up, officially, but it feels like I've lost her. My guilt over her losing her job at Clarke's is slowly swallowing me, and I even thought about talking to management though I know she'd hate that.

Axel came around yesterday asking what the hell was going on, and I've played it off, but he knew something was up when he learned Ainsley wasn't working at Clarke's anymore. He's read the different stories that have been published and seen the photos.

Ainsley and I went from perfect relationship to locked up and hiding while we let the pressure of it all come between us, even when we agreed to fight this together. We can only take so much, and I can't ask her for more than she's already done. Her private life has been put on display, strangers questioning her and taking photos when she's just trying to live her life.

Fortunately, I have my phone interview with Music & Life's editor today. She was quick to agree to the interview when Harris called her, knowing she was going to have an exclusive of the most desired information in our current society. All I can hope is that it will help guide people to learn the truth instead of assumptions.

I don't even want to show up to Nashville. I'm doing it for my fans. If it weren't for them, I would've dropped out of it. It wouldn't be the first time an artist had to take a step back and cancel an appearance. They would've found a replacement, but I owe my fans this last show. However, once I finish that performance tomorrow, I'll really be free from it all. No more expectations or appearances. I can go on my merry way, whatever path that leads. Hopefully, it includes Ainsley.

Bag packed with the basics and an outfit for the performance, I serve myself a scotch and watch the flames flicker in the fireplace. The guitar next to it catches my eye, and I stand to pick it up. A smirk appears on my face when I see the strap Ainsley got me. I run my finger over the wording, thinking back to the first time she told me about Frito pie. That woman wrapped me around her finger and kept me there.

I miss her.

I begin to play the song I've been working on, the same one she helped with. Eyes closed, my head bops as I fine-tune the music for the lyrics. Ainsley's smile appears behind my lids, the memory of her coming up with verses for the song playing in my mind. Her encouragement and support were evident as she expressed the confidence she had in me.

I continue to play the music on a loop until my phone rings. Placing the guitar next to me on the couch, I expel a deep breath and finish off my scotch. Here goes nothing. I answer the call, ready for my interview.

chapter 23

Ainsley

My phone lands on the sofa cushion with a thud after sending Knox my last text message. I scoop up a hefty amount of homemade cookie dough and take a bite. I meant to bake the cookies, but I had to have a taste of the dough. Next thing I knew, Knox was writing to me, and I was swallowing my woes one cookie dough serving at a time. These last couple of weeks have been hell, especially this last one.

When my manager at Clarke's said he had to speak to me, I was not expecting to get fired. I figured he'd have something to say about all the damn people coming into the bar, but I assumed he'd understand it wasn't my fault.

He did, but he also couldn't let it continue happening, and I can only guess the locals were starting to complain. I don't blame them, I also wish they didn't exist.

I especially hate the strain it's put on Knox and my relationship. I put more cookie dough into my mouth, fighting the tears. I'm in love with the man, and it's becoming painful to be with him. How does that even make sense? It doesn't.

I stroke the snowflake hanging from my neck, sighing. The tears I've trapped escape like a skilled ninja. I shake my head, chest vibrating as I catch my breath, and place the bowl with the dough on my coffee table.

I didn't feel this sad when I found out Bennett was cheating on me or when I moved out of the house we shared for a year, and Knox and I are still together. Albeit not in a great place, but he's still a part of my life. I did need some time, take a step back to clear my mind and get away from piercing looks and people forcing themselves into my life, thinking they have a right to know every detail. I also need to figure out what I'm going to do for an income. I can't just stay home, I need to work.

I lie on the couch in the fetal position and stare at the television without paying attention to what's showing. Silent tears stream down the side of my face. I have to trust Knox is working on a way to fix this, but I can't even begin to think how he could make them stop. The damage has been done.

His fans think I'm a home wrecker, the world sees me as someone out for his money. The only people who know the truth and haven't changed their opinion of me are his family and him. According to the world of entertainment, Ainsley Harding lured Knox in, gave him an ultimatum with his divorce, and demanded he stay in Wyoming instead of chase his dream to continue playing music. I've done none of that, only supporting him in any decision he feels is best for him.

I fell for the man none of these people know him as, who is far better than the idol they worship.

Ugh, then why did I tell him I needed space to be alone? God, these psychos are driving me crazy.

I look at the television screen, some random action movie playing, and I reach for the remote on the table, managing not to fall despite my refusal to sit up and grab it like a regular person. I stop when I see a Christmas movie and lean back on the couch, grabbing the bowl full of my current vice.

I moved to a small town like the woman in this movie. I fell for a local. Why can't my life be a Hallmark movie? Is that too much to ask for?

Okay, I've gone from sad and moody to crazy and ridiculous. I roll my eyes at myself and stuff my face until I have a sugar overload, and my heart is breaking even more thanks to my overactive mind. I can't see how Knox can actually fix this. Like, what do you tell heartless paparazzi that will suddenly make them surrender from all the juicy shit they think they're capturing?

You don't. They don't care. If they harass artists' children, then they don't care about a grown woman's feelings.

I huff and puff, but I have no solution. The worst part is that as much as I wanted to see him perform live, I knew it would be chaotic. I didn't want anything to interfere with his show or cause him stress in an already stressful moment. This is the last thing he has to do before truly cutting ties with his old label, and I want it to go smoothly. If I went with him to Nashville, the focus would be on us and not his amazing talent.

I glare at my phone when it rings, as if it interrupted the most important moment of my life. I look down at the half-empty bowl and sigh. It rings again, demanding my attention, and I reach for it.

"Hello?"

"Hi, sweetheart. I'm sorry to call you so late, but I wanted to make sure you were coming to dinner tomorrow."

"Hi Deb, I'm going to stay home actually. I appreciate it, so much, but I'm not really up to leaving the house." Knox's mom is a saint. She'd make the best mother-in-law. A cough strangles me, and I gasp for air as I try to gain my composure.

"Are you okay?"

"Yeah," it comes out muffled. I clear my throat. "Sorry, I don't know what happened," I lie because I know damn well I just choked on the idea of marrying Knox and having Deb as a mother-in-law.

"Drink some water," she suggests.

"Getting some right now." I stand, my unmatched socks warming my feet as I walk into the kitchen.

"Are you sure you don't want to come? You'll always have a setting on our table," she sounds worried.

"Yes, thank you." Between the snowy roads and my heartache, I rather stay home tomorrow night, dreaming of a New Year's kiss I won't get.

"If you change your mind—"

"Thanks, I'll let you know," I interrupt her.

"Good. I know things are difficult at the moment. Axel told me what happened at work, and I've seen all the nonsense they're saying about you, but I hope you know how much my son cares about you. I'll even risk and say he loves you," she confides.

"Loves?" My brows jump into my forehead.

Deb laughs softly. "I'm positive about it. Knox is trying to redo his life, and he's having a hard time with it even when he makes it seem like he has everything under control. I'm his mother, I know how challenging this is for him. He may not have always told me the truth," her voice becomes sad. "But I've never seen him care for someone the way he does for you. His marriage may have been a farce, but I want to believe it's helped him value people in his life more. The last thing he wants is to lose you."

I sniff, hearing her talk. "Thank you," my words tremble.

"I'm only sharing the truth. If you need us for anything, give us a call. I know Knox will be worried about your wellbeing while he's traveling."

"I appreciate that." I smile, grateful for her kindness and sincerity.

"Goodnight," she says, her voice so peaceful.

Unable to sleep, I sit back on the sofa and watch the rest of this stupid, romantic, funny movie I wish were my life.

♪

Oh, God, what am I going to do with my life? I pace the small space in my living room, baggy pajamas dragging.

My tips will only last so long, and I need to pay rent in a couple of days. I take a deep stabilizing breath, my heart still beating erratically. It's not like there are many options here for jobs. Besides, no one is going to want to hire me when I come with a stalking posse.

I start back on burning a trail into the carpet, my arms crossed. Yesterday, I was sad. Today, I'm freaking the fuck out. Good times.

Okay, Ainsley, you have a college degree. What can I do as a marketing specialist? I race to my room and grab my laptop. Looks like my New Year's Eve plans have turned into job searching and coming up with a life plan.

I wait for my screen to boot up, tapping my fingers on the section next to the touchpad.

I begin typing on Google, scanning the different jobs that appear in my search—none of them in Everton. I'd have to commute about an hour if I applied to any of these. Desperate times call for desperate measures, huh?

My head falls back, and I close my eyes. If it scared me to drive the short distance from my apartment to Clarke's in the snow, there's no way I'll feel comfortable driving an hour in this weather. Winter's just beginning.

I open another tab and do a different search. As long as I have a laptop and a phone, I can freelance. I can start up a website and create a social media account that's for a small business. We live in times where marketing is essential for anyone running a business, from a one-person company to a multi-million one—granted, those have a marketing team, but a girl can dream.

I extend my search on this, feeling like I may have a real plan. The notebook I grabbed in the middle of my career planning is filled out with notes, to-do lists, and possible contacts. Aim high and all that.

Taking a break, I check the time on my phone. Hmm… I haven't heard from Knox, and he should already be in Nashville. I can imagine he's been running around since he got there. They don't televise the Nashville event, so I won't even be able to watch him on TV.

Great, now I'm regretting not going. Hidden in my apartment, everything looks simple, though. As soon as I walk out of here, the buzz will start up again.

I warm up the canned chili, making dinner. Frito pie always makes bad days seem better, and it will now forever remind me of Knox. I sigh, stirring the chili to avoid it sticking to the pot. The bottle of The Macallan Knox bought so we could always have scotch when we stay in catches my eye. Hell to it, I grab a glass and serve myself a hefty serving. The amber liquid goes down smoothly while I wait for my dinner to finish warming up.

A bowl full of Fritos, chili, and topped with shredded cheese and sour cream sits on my small table and a refill of scotch next to it. I grab my phone and snap a photo, sending it to Knox.

Ainsley: good luck & enjoy it. thinking of you

I smile, hoping that chips away the tension. I savor my meal, responding to Axel when he asks if I'm really staying home on the last day of the year. I assure him I'm okay, and then check to see if Knox wrote back, although I know he didn't since I didn't get any notifications while I wrote to Axel. My chest falls with a sigh. I finish my dinner, my drink still full.

Might as well watch the Time Square celebration, even if they are two hours ahead of us. None of these are the musician I wish I were watching, but at least the music and chatter will distract me for a bit.

After a while, I check my phone again. There's still no response from Knox, and disappointment begins to swirl around me to the beat of the Jennifer Lopez song she's singing on the stage. I start to droop.

Opening Instagram, I do what any stalking girlfriend with FOMO would do—check his tags to see if anyone shared a short video clip of his performance. He should be done by now.

I see a video and watch the blurriness for fifteen seconds. Things may not be perfect at the moment, but I love that man. I haven't even told him yet with all the drama going on. I scroll to see more photos and pause.

What. The. Fuck.

I see a photo of him and Amelia hugging. I click on the image to read the caption. *Old flames reunited to kiss the year goodbye.*

I tilt my head, eyebrows furrowed. This can't be right. I scroll faster now and see another photo, this time they look like they're talking. I groan when I see the next photo is of Reese and Dex. Talk about the girlfriends of New Year's past. My heart sprints, my eyes are unsure if to burn with anger or shed tears.

I look for Amelia's Instagram account and check her tags. The same things appear on her side. Photos of her and Knox with assumptions of rekindling what was lost. One caption even says how he escaped my manipulations and went back to the woman he truly loves.

Dry laughter leaves my mouth. If they only knew.

However, he still hasn't responded to my message or called me all day. My hand goes to the snowflake around my neck, and I'm tempted to yank it. Instead, I rub it gently as I see a still image of Knox on stage, the guitar strap I gave him around his shoulders. A sad smile takes over, and I release a slow breath.

Is this how it all ends?

I could torture myself and search his name for all of the internet to share their gossip with me, or I could wait until he gets back and talk to him like a mature adult.

I've always considered myself mature, which is why I don't understand when my fingers begin typing his name on my phone browser of their own accord. This is one rabbit hole I'm going to regret getting lost in.

chapter 24

Ainsley

Pounding.

Mmm… Are those fireworks?

"Ainsley."

What the hell? I turn on the couch and grip the back cushion as I hit the floor with a thud. "Ouch." I rub my lower back and stretch my arms over my head, an unattractive yawn filling my face.

"Are you in there?" The same pounding and muffled voice that woke me up sounds again, and I might kill someone. I rub my eyes and walk to the door.

Knox's body visibly relaxes when I swing open the door.

"What are you doing here?" My half-slumber state is still trying to remember what day it is.

"I wanted to give you a New Year's kiss." He smirks a stupid sexy smirk, before leaning in.

My hand automatically goes to his chest to stop him. New Year's Eve. Nashville. Amelia. I take a step back and cross my arms.

"What's wrong?" the words rush out of his mouth, and his hands go into his hair.

"You tell me," I demand. "I saw photos of you and Amelia in Nashville. Was it nice to cozy up with her?" I arch a brow.

"Fuck." He blows out a puff of air. "It's not like that. You of all people should know not to believe what they say. Yes, I saw her. The photos are real. She called Harris to let him know she was in Nashville to talk to me. I told her to fuck off until she said she wanted to talk to me about making things right for you and me."

He reaches for my hand. "Can I come in?"

"It's better than having this conversation out in the hall where psychos who don't have family that cares about them are lingering, waiting to catch us." I say this louder than necessary in case anyone really is hiding in the hallway can hear me.

Knox chuckles at my words and walks in.

"You have to listen to me, okay?" He walks into the living room without an invitation, his body shadowing the place. "Amelia came to see me before the show. She was actually hoping to meet you. It felt like the Amelia from years ago when she was normal."

I don't like the sound of that. Could this be an Amelia he can fall in love with?

"Anyway," his hand rubs the back of his neck, his fidgeting driving me crazy. "She came to see me to tell me she fired her publicist and was going to release a statement revealing the truth about our marriage. She'll deal with the consequences."

"What?" My hand lifts to my mouth.

Knox nods. "She's going to risk it. Actually, she already did." He grabs his phone, typing something, and then turns it around for me to read. My eyes skim the text, widening. She did it.

"She also scheduled the exclusive with Music & Life, so the editor thought she was getting a double whammy when I had told her I wanted an interview. I didn't share the truth, but Amelia did, and they did a double spread for both of us online tonight. It will be in print tomorrow morning." He's still tense, waiting for me to react.

"But..." I scratch my forehead and furrowed brows. "Why did she do this?"

"She wasn't always a diva. Besides, she finally had her chance to be with CJ, and her publicist was refusing her to make it public. It would've taken away from her victim role in this divorce and dulled out the rumors about you and me," he shrugs as if it's no big deal. It's a huge freaking deal.

"But I saw the posts on Instagram, and none of them say this," I point out.

"It will take a few hours for it to catch wind, and those photos were taken before anything was made public. They saw us and assumed we were getting back together."

"Why is this so complicated? Why can't people mind their own?" I ask almost to myself.

"Because people feed off the drama. It nourishes their egos." He's never been more right about something.

"Can I ask you something?" I lift my gaze to meet his, struggling to hold the eye contact while I ask what's coming.

"Always."

I take a deep breath and let it go, reeling in my emotions. "Did you see Reese?" I tuck my lips into my teeth.

"I did," he nods. "You have nothing to worry about." His hands find my hips, and he tugs until I'm standing closer to him. "Ainsley, I'm crazy in love with you. I saw her, and I smiled, seeing how happy she was. And all I could think was, thank you because I never would've met you had she been unhappy. You're the only person I want. I know everything's been a mess, but things will get better. Now that people know what really went on between Amelia and me, there won't be much to hang on to in terms of spinning a web of lies.

"People will still be curious about us, but that's a given as long as I'm in the public eye. I promise, though, it will be more curiosity about our relationship than tearing us apart."

"How are you so sure?" I lean back a bit and tilt my head up.

"Because we're a normal couple. Eventually, they'll get bored of us," he chuckles.

My eyes widen, "Will you?"

"Nah. You," he cups my face, "have breathed life back into me. You've given me sunshine and hope, and you've helped revive my passion and dreams," he smiles.

"So, you're really in love with me?" I bite down my smile.

"Crazy in love," he corrects.

"Well, I guess it's a good thing I'm crazy in love with you if not that'd be embarrassing for you." I shake my head as seriously as I can be and pat his chest, but the man I love just confessed he loves me, too, so my smile is split open. I can't even hide it.

Knox leans in, stopping an inch from my lips. "Happy New Year," his lips brush against mine.

"Happy New Year," I repeat, molding our mouths together, gripping the lapels of his leather jacket before looping my arms around his neck. His tongue swipes mine, the feel of being in his arms refilling a piece of my heart. It's been too long since we've been like this—no barriers or tension marring our time together.

"Are you hungry?" I ask, breaking away. "I have left over Frito pie, which you would know if you hadn't ignored my text message." I step back and cross my arms, lifting an accusatory eyebrow.

"Sorry, but I saw it when we landed. The service was terrible at the event with all the machines and technology running at the same time. By the time I saw it, I was already racing over to talk to you in person."

"Next time, call me." I make sure he knows how important it is to me. "I was breaking here after seeing those photos and even before with everything that was going on between us."

"You're right. I'm sorry. I was focused on performing and getting back, I didn't think," he searches my face. For the first time in a few weeks, I feel like we are back on track.

"Now, about that meal," a devilish smile brightens his face.

"Frito pie, the best comfort food," I tilt my head and smile.

"I was thinking of eating something else." I squeal when he lifts my body, catching me off guard, and runs his lips down my neck. I moan into the room and rock my hips against his.

"Baby…" he groans. "You. I'm going to eat you." His words come out forced.

I lean into his ear. "Best meal you'll ever have," I whisper before taking his lobe into my mouth and sucking.

"Fuck," he growls and takes us into my bedroom. "Get naked," he demands as soon as my feet hit the floor.

"You mean, you don't want to keep me in my sexy pajamas?" I motion down my baggy clothes.

Knox laughs and shakes his head. "I love you in anything, but right now I want you naked."

I take my time, stripping out of my frumpy pajamas, wondering how the hell he thinks I look sexy right now. When my pants drop, and he realizes I'm not wearing underwear, his eyes squeeze closed as he takes control of his breathing.

I sit on the bed and scoot back, leaning up on my elbows with a raised eyebrow, challenging him. Wordlessly, his weight presses onto me as his lips smash against mine. Before I can deepen the kiss, he snickers and travels down my body, pausing at my breasts, taking turns as he pulls each nipple into his mouth, teasing me. I squirm beneath him, and his smile spreads against my skin, his beard tickling my sensitive body.

He looks up at me when he stops at my pelvis, nipping my skin with a mischievous smile. My teeth pull my bottom lip in, and my entire body fills with goosebumps. He's so close to where I want to feel him. I push my hips up, and his hands grab them, keeping them pinned to the mattress.

"Tease," I moan quietly.

As a response, his tongue swipes up my pussy, making me cry out. "Call me a tease one more time."

"Tease," I don't back down and buck my hips when he runs his tongue over me again, sucking my clit into his mouth.

"Holy shit," I scream and grip the sheets beside me.

"Call out my name, babe." His words vibrate against me, adding to the sensation that is quickly leading me down Orgasmville.

I pull his hair and press his head down as his tongue works its magic on my body. My nerve-endings are begging for a release, and my entire body is shaking as he continues his relentless attack. Sweet, sweet torture.

I moan, crying out his name on repeat, as my toes curl and my thighs squeeze his upper body. My orgasm shakes me, rolling waves of desire that knock me stupid as I only focus on riding my climax.

He finally stops when my body goes limp. "Delicious." He licks his lips, and I think I just orgasmed a second time watching him do that.

"That was…" I try to catch my breath. I should work out so I can keep up with him.

Knox chuckles, lifting himself over me and kissing me. "Good?" he raises his eyebrows.

"No, better than good. Amazing." I pull him down, kissing him. "Get naked," I demand against his lips the same way he did to me earlier.

"Yes, ma'am." He stands, removing his leather jacket and then his plaid, button-down shirt, tossing them both on the floor as he toes off his boots. His jeans drop, followed by his boxer briefs. He runs a hand up and down his cock, my gaze glued to the movement.

I stand from the bed, moving his hand and replacing it with mine. "I won't last," he mumbles.

"Shhh…" I keep moving up and down his length, feeling empowered as he grows in my hand. I guide him to sit on the bed, and his hands immediately go to my hips. I wiggle in his hold and wink before straddling him.

"I'm on the pill," I state, clear about my intentions.

He makes a sound I've never heard before, crossed between a lion and a wolf.

"I love you," he grabs my head and crashes our mouths together. "Make love to me however you want."

"You're sure?" I try to gain control of my desire to make sure we're both on the same page.

"Never been more certain of anything in my life," he responds.

His words, mixed with love and assurance, wash over me, and I lift my body. Aligning us, I lower myself on Knox, both of us exhaling audibly.

"You feel so good," he says through clenched teeth.

"I know." I nod, giving myself a chance to take this all in before lowering the rest of the way until he's filling me completely. This is the first time I have ever made love to someone without a condom, and the feeling is night and day when you don't have a barrier—physically or emotionally.

Needing to feel all of him, I begin to move, his hands supporting my hips. I find his lips, kissing him with wild abandon as our bodies move together. I moan into his kiss as my nipples brush against his chest, adding to the overload of feelings taking over. Knox speeds us up, lifting my body and letting me drop back down, harder and harder. Every part of his body that touches mine adds to my release. My head falls back as I call out, a second orgasm rushing through me.

Mid-orgasm, Knox stands, still inside of me, and turns us around as he starts pounding into me, chasing his own climax and extending mine.

"Oh God," my words are barely audible as my mouth hangs open and I stare into his brown eyes, also laced with desire.

By the time we both come down, my body is lax.

"Make me one promise," I whisper, running a hand through Knox's hair.

"Of course," he looks at me as he twists us, so we're lying next to each other, still inside of me.

"We ring in every New Year like this," I smile, a fool in love.

"I wouldn't do it any other way," he promises, kissing my forehead.

chapter 25

Knox

I finish my call with Harris and walk into my bedroom to see Ainsley is already awake. "Good morning," she says when I walk in.

I climb on the bed next to her and pull her into my arms, my lips finding hers. "Mornin', had to take a call from Harris," I explain.

"That's okay. Everything is good?" She lifts a brow.

"More than." Thankfully, as soon as word got around about Amelia's confession and my interview a week ago, things quieted down. They even offered Ainsley her job back at Clarke's, which she gratefully declined.

"What did he think of the idea?" She looks up at me through mussed, blonde hair.

"He's on board." I smile, finally having some grip on my life. I got a couple of calls from other labels when the news broke, but I won't be signing with any of them. This time, I'm doing things my way.

"This is so exciting. We're both starting new journeys in our careers." The sheet falls as Ainsley sits up, exposing her bare chest. I groan and lean in, licking her puckered nipple.

Ainsley giggles and moans at the same time, fingers combing through the back of my hair, my dick taking notice of her nails scraping my scalp.

"We have plans," she whispers, however, not moving my head away.

"We can be late," I scrape my teeth before moving to her other nipple, and I'll bet every dollar I own that her pussy's wet for me. I move my hand down and groan when I feel her soaked through.

"Babe…" I look up and see dilated pupils drowning the blue in her eyes.

"I can't wait," I murmur before I work her body like a vintage guitar, perfect and in-tune with her needs. Right before she climaxes, I move her onto my body and thrust into her. She cries out something I can't make out and don't bother trying to decipher as I get lost in her body. When her nails scratch my chest, I pull her mouth down to mine and kiss her with every ounce of need as our movements become erratic.

I should be ashamed it doesn't take long for us to finish, but the truth is, this woman riles me up by just being herself. She's foreplay without laying a hand on me.

"Well, I guess you really couldn't wait," Ainsley says on a giggle, my cock still inside of her.

"I don't joke when it comes to you."

Her hand comes to my face. "And I love that about you. As much as I rather stay here with you the rest of the day, we do need to go." I slap her ass, and she moans. "You do that again, I won't let you slip out of me." I want to make her keep that promise, but I know this is important for her—and I have some self-control.

"Love you," I kiss the tip of her nose. "Go take a shower."

She carefully lifts her body and stands. Before she walks into the en suite bathroom, she looks at me over her shoulder, "Love you, too." I stare as her naked body disappears behind the door and lie back, arms behind my head with a proud smile on my face.

I may have thought I wouldn't find another woman who made me feel this way again, but life threw Ainsley my way and challenged me to keep my distance. I love her like I've never loved anyone, even the person I thought I would spend my life with. Everything I lived gave me a different perspective. It taught me to appreciate the people in my life and my relationships. Without that, as much as I hate to admit it, I probably wouldn't be where I am right now.

"I'll dry my hair in here so you can shower," Ainsley interrupts my thoughts when she walks out of the bathroom wrapped in a towel.

"Fine, but this afternoon we're spending it alone." I stand and catch her eyes travel down my body. I pause when I reach her and kiss her lips. "You can stare all you want, I'm all yours."

"Go shower," she whispers with a small smile and wink, but she doesn't hide her gawking as I walk away from her, tilting her head to catch my backside when I look over my shoulder.

"Sexy," she teases.

I jump in the shower, needing to break away before I do keep her to myself. After the last few weeks, I love having her here, being herself again. Now I need to get her to move in with me. I come up with a plan while I get ready. After this meeting we have today, I think I might be able to talk her into it.

♪

I watch as Ainsley handles herself like a seasoned professional and wise marketer. When she approached The Mad Batter, offering her services as a freelance marketing specialist, it didn't take long for Mrs. Engle to call her with a few questions.

Apparently, she's been wanting to break into the online market to sell her desserts and pastries and hasn't known which direction to take. Ainsley has brought up great options, along with examples of similar businesses that run online shops and how to package the food, so it doesn't perish.

"If you have any questions, please don't hesitate to call me," Ainsley says with joy.

"Thank you. I'll look through my budget and call you. I know the beginning will be a little tight, but I think this is a great way to expand my business and make extra income," Mrs. Engle smiles warmly.

"It definitely is additional income. With a solid plan, you'll have orders coming in without even trying," Ainsley assures her.

"Thank you again. We'll be in touch." They stand and shake hands. I follow suit, shaking Mrs. Engle's hand as well.

I wrap my arm around Ainsley's shoulder as we leave the shop, but she stops me. "Can I have two mini bundt cakes?" she asks Mrs. Engle.

"Of course, dear."

Ainsley looks up and leans into me. My arm drops around her waist, kissing the top of her head and tap the top of her thigh. I place a hand over hers when she reaches for her wallet.

"I'm paying," I tell her with no room for argument.

"Knox…" The stubborn woman still tries to convince me otherwise.

When I lift my eyebrows, she nods and thanks me, knowing it's a losing battle.

"You're the best," she holds me by the waist. "Where to now?"

Wanting to spend some time outdoors, I ask her, "Do you know how to ride a horse?"

Ainsley laughs as if I asked her if she wanted to go swimming in freezing weather. "I can't ski, what makes you think I can control a horse?"

"Good. I was hoping that'd be your answer. Guess you'll have to ride with me, make sure you hold on tight," I wink.

"You really want to ride? Now? In this snow?" Her arms motion around her as if I hadn't noticed the weather outside.

"Yes, trust me." I link our fingers and head to my truck. "You did great in there, by the way. I'm really proud." She's a natural, and it's clear she loves what she does. I understand needing to take a step back from your career and figure things out, but I'm glad she came back to her chosen path.

"Thank you. I feel like I did when I first graduated and started working. It's exciting to get ideas rolling and putting my creativity to work. Granted, I'm running my own business as well, so I'll have to balance everything, but it's more fulfilling when you're doing it for yourself." Walking down the sidewalk, her steps are light, and her entire body is bright and happy. She has an energy I'm glad is in my life.

"Don't I know it." I nod, excited for my own new project.

"You're really excited about Bentley Records, huh?" She gives me a knowing smile.

"Yeah, especially after talking to Harris this morning. He's flying out next week, so we can meet and go over details in person." This will be an entirely different approach than I've taken in the past, and I hope that my name and following will help with the transition.

First, I'm writing the songs I want, and I'm not going to rush to put a record out. I also want to start with smaller shows, reach the fans more intimately.

I've already made plans to convert part of my basement into a studio, making my gym smaller. It's not like I need that much space to work out.

I drive us toward the ranch, ready to go for a ride with my number one girl and eat these Bundt cakes.

We're sitting atop one of the fences where we paused to eat dessert after riding Ty for a bit, looking out into the mountains and miles of snow covering the land. I don't need much more than this—fresh air and my girl's arms around me as we ride.

"Sing it for me," Ainsley asks, her eyes soft as she gives me that lopsided smile. Can't say no to that.

"I don't have my guitar," I state the obvious.

"It's okay, we can hum the beat. Well, I can, and you can sing even if I'm not great at staying with the tune. You're a pro, so you can use your skills to make it work," she rambles on, and I laugh.

"Ready?" I wink. She nods with a megawatt smile, and what would only be called heart-eyes in an emoji-ruling world.

I clear my throat and hum the opening tune before I start singing.

Dark streets swallowing me in
As I walked blind,
I didn't know which way to go
Or who to trust,
But then I met you

Your touch warmed my skin
And sparked my life,
Your smile shone on me
Another way to live

You've made it easy,
Sweeping me away
And making me believe

In more than heartache

You make it easy to love
When I promised I'd never
Open up to another

I get lost in your eyes,
Blue and wild,
As your smile
Shines a new light into my life

You've made it easy,
Sweeping me away
And making me believe
In more than heartache

I plan to spend my life
Winning your heart,
Proving what you mean to me
When the lights go out
And it's just you and me

You've made it easy,
Sweeping me away,
Sweeping me away

Ainsley whispers the words along with me, already memorizing the song I finished while on my trip to Nashville. She's had me practicing it each day. Her astonishment as I sing is evident on her face.

"I really love that song," she sighs.

"You should since it's about you," I tell her what she already knows, and her cheeks turn pink. She pulls on her beanie, doing anything to keep her busy.

I grab her hands and look into her eyes. "I actually wanted to talk to you about something."

Her nose wrinkles and her eyebrows furrow the tiniest bit. "What's wrong?"

"Nothing." I shake my head. "This is good stuff." I run my thumb over her gloved hand.

"Stop stalling," her shoulders lift close to her ears. I massage them, beckoning them to relax.

"I want you to move in with me."

Ainsley looks at me, her face expressionless except for her eyeballs shifting back and forth between mine.

"Hello?" My eyes open wider, heart starting to race.

"It's too soon." Her eyes blink quickly. "Right?"

"No. One, I love you, and I have no doubt you're the woman I'm going to marry one day. Two, when I bought my house, I always envisioned sharing it with someone. Three, time means nothing when you're sure of the person by your side. I'm a million percent positive you're the woman I'll always love. I want Frito pie nights and snowball fights. I want to sit by the fire at the end of the day, share our dreams with each other and celebrate our accomplishments."

We spend almost every night together. There's no point in keeping two homes. I'm ready for this. I've never been more prepared to live my life with someone as I am right now. She comes first, and I can't imagine it being any other way.

"Frito pie nights and snowball fights? How do I turn that down?" She pinches her lips together and runs her fingers across her chin as if she's contemplating this.

"You don't. Say yes." I ghost my lips over hers. Her giggles meet my lips.

"Okay, yes." Her hands squeeze my face, and she smashes her lips on mine, almost sending us over the fence we're sitting on.

"Fuck yeah," I holler into the wind. Ainsley laughs, her entire body shaking.

"I'm gonna marry you someday," I promise.

"You better," she winks.

Just when I thought my life was ruined, and I had come to a dead end, life made me stumble into this stunning woman's path. She's light, happiness, and peace. She's made me believe in more than mistakes and guilt. She pulled me out of the hole I was digging myself into, without realizing she was doing it. Simply by being herself, Ainsley saved me. She gave me something to look forward to and helped me believe in myself again— not as a musician, but as a man.

I'm looking forward to the rest of my life with her.

epilogue

Ainsley

five months later

I tiptoe to the studio in the basement, hoping I get to catch a glimpse of Knox singing before he sees me. I finished working on the tasks I had pending for The Mad Batter and thought I'd come down here. Ever since Mrs. Engle agreed to work with me, her online store grew exponentially in a short time. Other small businesses started contacting me to work together. It's been amazing to help locals and do something I love.

I lean my ear against the door of the studio, concentrating so I can hear something. Sometimes I wish the studio wasn't soundproof, although I understand why it is.

These last five months have been amazing. Living with someone always takes some getting used to, and Knox and I have had our moments but nothing impossible to work through.

He's everything I've ever dreamed of in a man, and he supports me unconditionally.

I stumble forward when the door opens and catch Harris's laughing eyes.

"You've got a visitor," he winks at me. "I'll be back in a bit." He grabs his coat and leaves me alone with Knox.

"Were you spying on us?" He reaches for me from his place on the sofa in here, and I willingly go to him.

"I wanted to listen to you singing," I admit.

"You can always ask me to sing for you." I stand between his legs and bend my head to drop a kiss on his lips.

"It's a beautiful day," I state. "And I finished working early."

"What do you want to do?" he asks.

"Let's go for a walk when you finish with Harris," I suggest, loving spring in Wyoming.

"We were talkin' actually, and we need someone to help us with marketing," his words trail off. I know where he's going with this. Since he and Harris started working the label, he's been asking me to work with him. I continue to shoot down the idea, but he's a persistent man. Regardless, I shake my head. I love him too much to get involved in this. I help him when I can, even working on songs with him. That's my favorite.

"Work with me. You have the marketing expertise, and I need a marketing team for the label," he doesn't hold back.

"I love you, but no," I shake my head and straddle him.

"Why not?" He runs his hands up and down my back, causing me to shiver.

"Because working together can cause problems, and I don't want problems with you. I want Frito pie nights and snowball fights," I tell him the same way he did months ago when he asked me to move in with him.

"Fine," he sighs. "Then, marry me."

I stop midway to kissing him, frozen. "What?" I stutter.

"Marry me. I want to spend the rest of my life with you. I want to laugh and hold you, make love to you. There's no one else I'd want by my side, supporting me and loving me."

"Oh, my God, you're serious." I'm still gripping his face, and he chuckles.

"So serious, I even got a ring." He pushes his hand into his back pocket, lifting us a bit as he reaches behind him.

Knox leans back on the sofa, leaving some space between us to open the box. A solitaire diamond shines back at me.

"Hard_Ains, there's no one else I want to rap to Eminem with, write songs with, and hold throughout the night. Marry me," his words are soft, his demand coming out more like a question.

"Well, if you bought a ring, it'd be rude to say no, huh?" I give him a crooked smile and smash my lips against his, loosening my hold on his face. "I love you," I say against his lips.

"I love you, too." His mouth takes over, controlling the kiss.

When he breaks the kiss, leaving us both breathless, he slips the ring on my finger. "You've made me the happiest man on this planet every day since I met you. I hope to make you as happy as you've made me."

"You already do." He has no idea how much I love him. He was a welcomed surprise when I met him in the fall, curiosity about the infamous Knox Bentley already filling me before he walked into Clarke's.

As soon as I saw his hidden smile, I knew there was more to him than what he showed to the world.

"After all, you are the chili to my Frito pie," I tell him my cheesy line.

His laugh shakes his body, and he cups my face to kiss me again. I know our adventure is just beginning and we've got miles to travel together in this life.

Axel and Lia's story follows Write You a Love Song. Curious about the woman Axel ran into at Clarke's? Continue reading for a sneak peek of Roping Your Heart.

sneak peak

roping your heart

"You're somethin' else," I shake my head, teasing her. I met Ainsley when she first moved here in the fall, and instantly connected with her. She didn't know anyone, and I felt protective of her. I wanted to make sure she felt welcomed, and I know some people in town can be hesitant about giving new people a chance.

Knox returns with a large amount of cotton candy spun around the paper cone.

"Whoa," Ainsley perks up and takes a piece of the candy. "So good. Thanks, babe." She lifts on her toes and kisses him. I look away from their exchange, sweeter than that damn candy they're eating, and look out at the crowd again.

My eyes land on her, hand clutching her stomach as she laughs. Her tanned skin makes her green eyes brighter as her long hair sways in its ponytail. Lia always lit up any room she was in with her joy, even outside she lights up everything around her without the help of the sun.

"You still haven't made a move?" Ainsley giggles next to me as she teases.

I glare at her and finish my beer.

"I'll take that as a no," her head bobs from side to side as she lifts her eyebrows.

"Don't you have a wedding to obsess over instead of my love life?"

"You know I'm a simple gal." She bumps her shoulder with my arm, not quite reaching my shoulder, and I chuckle.

"You're the best sister-in-law."

"Clearly," she lifts on hand, palm facing up, just like that girl emoji on our phones.

"Humble, too," I joke and look back out at the crowd, no longer seeing Lia where she was standing.

"Are you afraid it will ruin your friendship?" Ainsley whispers, all joking disappearing from her tone.

"I'm not afraid. I know we're both on the same page, but I haven't found the right timing," I confess, squeezing the plastic cup between my fingers until a loud crack sounds.

"I personally think that timing is an excuse we use to postpone acting on our emotions. If I thought the timing with Knox was wrong because of his divorce, I wouldn't be here right now," she shrugs.

"She's got a point, bro." Knox finally speaks up. I almost forgot he was standing with us.

"Heck yeah, I do." Ainsley wraps an arm around Knox's waist and smiles up at him. She's right.

"You guys want a beer?" I ask them, eyeing the beer stand a few feet away.

"Sure," they say in unison.

I grab three beers, and when I turn around I see Lia talking to Ainsley and Knox.

"Hey," I smile over at Lia and hand Knox and Ainsley their cups. "You want a beer?"

"Thanks, but I've got one." She lifts a cup from the other side. "This parade is always the best part of the year."

"I have to agree," I nod.

"I'm excited to see these floats. From what I hear, the competition gets intense," Ainsley comments, looking around to the street where the parade will take place.

"You have no idea," Lia laughs. "Remember when we participated in one," she looks at me.

"We got kicked out," I add as I guffaw. Lia's head goes back as her laughter becomes wilder.

"It was so bad." She clutches her side and takes a deep breath before continuing. "We wanted to see what all the fuss was about, so we joined one of the teams. They were militant when it came to meeting and building that thing, but we weren't as committed. They eventually kicked us out of the team and banned us for life." Lia wipes under her eyes. "I wonder if they'd let us back in now as adults," she adds in amusement.

Ainsley begins to laugh with her. "Are they that serious about it?" The ridiculousness ringing in her voice.

"Yes," Lia nods fervently with wide eyes. "And don't you dare question their passion for it," she warns Ainsley in a low voice. "It's a sure-fire way to get all of Everton on your bad side."

"Gotcha." Ainsley nods her head once and zips her lips with her fingers. "It sounds like you guys had a blast growing up," she comments.

"We sure did." Lia looks up at me with a smile. "Sometimes I had to talk him down from crazy ideas."

"Me? I'm pretty sure you were the one that thought it was smart to break into Glenn High and steal their uniforms." I point my finger at her but chuckle seeing the humor shadowing her face.

"Best idea ever." Lia claps her hands with pride.

"Was that your high school?" Ainsley's eyebrows knit together.

"Nope, that's the high school in the town over and our biggest rival. We had the basketball championship the next day," Knox explains, lifting his eyebrows at both Lia and me. "When they ran out with a bag full of jerseys, Axel's truck was stuck in the mud. I had to go bail them out, and they left the bag with jerseys on the ground while making a run for it."

"You always did have our backs," Lia holds in her laughter, knowing more than once Knox had to cover for us.

"I'm just glad you both grew up," he shakes his head, grinning.

"I would've loved to grow up in a town like this," Ainsley sighs and looks around the square wistfully.

"You're here now," Lia smiles. "Trust me, no matter how old you are, this town always has something to do."

"I've noticed that," Ainsley responds, leaning her head on Knox's shoulder.

Lia looks at me with a smile and lifts the cup to her lips. I want to hold her, pull her to my side, and keep her in my life forever. Nothing standing in our way now.

♪

Can't wait for the next Fabiola Francisco book?

Follow her on her website:
www.authorfabiolafrancisco.com

acknowledgments

First and foremost, thank you so much for taking the time to read Write You a Love Song. This is a story that I knew I had to write when I first wrote Knox's character in Promise You. There are always two sides to every story, and it was so fun to explore his side. Ainsley is the perfect woman to help him overcome his past, his guilt, and give him hope for new love. Your support means the world to me, and like I've said before, without you this all wouldn't be possible.

To the team of people, whom without this this book would not be complete—Claire and Wendy from Bare Naked Words, Amy from Q Designs, Joy and Ally from Happily Ever Insta, Bex from Editing Ninja, and Cary for the beautiful formatting. Thank you ladies for being a part of this book and helping me make this release the best it can be.

Christy and Rachel, no matter the years that pass or the amount of books we write (or now the miles and miles that separate us), I know that you two are always there for me. I can't thank you enough for that. #soapythighsforlife

Brittany, Cary, and Ashley, thanks for your encouragement, chats, and venting moments. It means a lot to know I can count on you when it comes to writing books and living life.

Veronica and Miriam, you've been there from the beginning and still put up with my book conversations. lol Thank you!

Ally, you have been a lifesaver when it comes to this series. Thank you for beta reading, giving me feedback, responding to my messages at any and every hour, and basically listening to me ramble. lol Axel is yours!

Joy, you're my boo. I'm pretty sure I'd be more of a mess than I am without you. You say I don't need to thank you, but this is my book, so I'm thanking you for all you do. Even if we're only chatting about air conditioning temperatures, I know I can count on you. Seventy degrees is still the perfect temperature.

To all the bloggers, authors, and bookstagrammers that have shared my work and supported me, thank you. It takes a village, and you are all a part of mine.

about the author

Fabiola Francisco loves the simplicity—and kick—of scotch on the rocks. She follows Hemingway's philosophy—write drunk, edit sober. She writes women's fiction and contemporary romance, dipping her pen into new adult and young adult. Her moods guide her writing, taking her anywhere from sassy and sexy romances to dark and emotion-filled love stories.

Writing has always been a part of her life, penning her own life struggles as a form of therapy through poetry. She still stays true to her first love, poems, while weaving longer stories with strong heroines and honest heroes. She aims to get readers thinking about life and love while experiencing her characters' journeys.

She is continuously creating stories as she daydreams. Her other loves are country music, exploring the outdoors, and reading.